HANGING HOUSE

An Emmie Rose Haunted Mystery Book 1

DEAN RASMUSSEN

Hanging House: An Emmie Rose Haunted Mystery Book 1

Dean Rasmussen

For more information about this book, visit:

www.deanrasmussen.com
dean@deanrasmussen.com

Hanging House: An Emmie Rose Haunted Mystery Book 1

Published by:

Dark Venture Press, 15502 Stoneybrook West Parkway, Suite 104-452, Winter Garden, FL 34787

Cover Art: Mibl Art

Developmental Editor: C.B. Moore

Line Editor: C.B. Moore

❀ Created with Vellum

NINETEEN YEARS AGO

Someone had built Emmie's house in two sections, and she loved it. Her family occupied the front half and all the upstairs bedrooms. Frankie and his mom lived in the lower-back half. Two sandwiched doors separated their areas, and when their parents opened them, allowing them to run freely between the two sections, it was like a portal into another world.

The doors were open now, and Frankie ran into his part of the house gripping the pack of cards. He stopped to play the game, pulling one card from the deck and covering it with his palm.

Emmie paused. "The Hermit."

Frankie flipped the card over and stared at it. He looked up at Emmie through narrow eyes. "You cheated."

"I didn't cheat. That's ridiculous."

"You can't guess it right every time."

"Why not?"

"Because then it's cheating. Nobody guesses it right every time."

"Do you want me to lie?"

Frankie glanced around and behind himself as he inched away from her. "We're going to try this again." He took three giant steps back and pressed the cards flat against his chest. "You can't see them now, right?"

"I can't see which one you're going to pick. No."

"Turn around." Frankie swirled his finger in the air.

Emmie groaned and turned away from him, facing the doorway that led into her family's side of the house. Her parents were in the kitchen blabbing on about something super boring. The television blared in the living room, but nobody watched it. The sun poured in through the unshaded windows along the front of the house and glared off the floorboards.

Frankie grinned. "Okay, try to guess it now."

Emmie smirked. "I already know what it is."

"What is it then?"

"The Fool."

Frankie sneered. "You're cheating!"

"No, I'm telling the truth. I'm not cheating at all."

"You have to be. Nobody guesses it right every time."

"I do."

"Okay then, I'll go hide somewhere, and after I'm in my hiding spot, I'll pick a card. That way you can't cheat."

Emmie rolled her eyes.

"*And* I'm going to time you again." Frankie pulled out a stopwatch from his pocket. His mother had purchased it for him on his birthday a few days earlier, so he could keep track of his own swimming records. "Let's see how long you take now to find me *and* guess the card."

"All right." Emmie groaned.

"Ready? Go stand over there and face the wall." Frankie rushed forward and pushed her over to a little corner next to the

TV stand. He turned her toward the wall and stepped back. "You can't see me now, can you?"

"No, I see a wall." *And some cracks and a spider web.*

"Okay, good, now don't you dare peek."

"Fine."

Frankie rushed away, and the echoes of his feet pounding across the hardwood floors echoed through the house until they faded to muffled thumps. Emmie began the count from ten to one.

Even without her Third Eye, she still knew where he would go. Down to the basement. But after he reached the bottom of the stairs, she lost the thumping of his feet.

She tried *not* to see him. She really did. It was more fun that way. She avoided shutting her eyes for longer than a blink, when her Third Eye would reveal his location as a blurry image of light against the blackness of her eyelids. She would play fair and not see him this time. Play the game like everyone else. Like a *normal* kid.

When she finished counting down from ten to one, she took off toward the basement, charging through the house with her heart pounding. She stomped down the stairs, pausing a moment on the last step to listen for any sounds of Frankie. The cool basement air invigorated her after playing upstairs for so long.

Emmie turned left into the larger section of the basement. Larger, but not empty. She looped around stacks of boxes, discarded items and old toys. She paused. "I know you're down here."

No sound from Frankie. She looked behind a stack of red plastic totes labeled "Christmas stuff" and hurried into a small room her dad used to store his "souvenirs." Shelves displayed the many creepy figurines, pentagrams, wooden masks, photos, devil's heads, skulls, and a Ouija board. All the items she wasn't allowed to play with unless she asked. She never asked.

She glanced inside. Not many places to hide in there, and one dark corner at the far side of the room. Frankie would never go back there, anyway.

Shutting the door, she circled around more scattered items that revealed nothing. Only one place left to hide—the bathroom. Emmie opened the door and knew right away he was in there somewhere because the light was on. Frankie would never hide in the darkness for long. She took one step further and spotted the top edge of his shirt in the bathtub. She held back a laugh.

Her shoes tapped against the floor as she tiptoed over to him, each step revealing more of his clothes until she reached out and tapped Frankie's shoulder. "Found you!"

Frankie growled. "How come you found me so fast? You followed me."

"I didn't."

Frankie clicked the top button on his stopwatch and stood up. "It took you two minutes and thirty-five seconds to find me."

"I can probably beat that."

"I bet you can't." He stepped out of the bathtub. "You stay down here and count to ten. I'll go hide somewhere good this time. You'll never find me. No cheating."

Frankie started his stopwatch and Emmie sighed as he took off up the stairs.

"Ten, nine, eight..." Emmie continued counting and stepped out of the bathroom.

Her dad's tools surrounded her, along with other scattered possessions. A multitude of electronic devices lay in piles around his workbench against the far wall. Her dad loved to fix things— sometimes he got them working again, sometimes not. But when something *did* work, he'd make a big deal out of it.

Months earlier, he had revived an old pinball machine after spending weeks piecing it back together. The finished machine looked nothing like the original pile of junk he'd carried down in boxes. At the time, it had seemed so pointless to assemble a thousand different little things. How could her dad keep track of it all? But it slowly came together, and it worked, although now it sat in the corner untouched, hidden beneath a couple of cardboard boxes.

Frankie's footsteps above her faded away. He'd gone back into their apartment.

She finished counting and yelled out, "Ready or not, here I come."

She doubted Frankie could hear her down in the basement, but she didn't want to be accused of not following the rules again.

As she crossed the basement toward the stairs, something ahead caught her eye. She slowed.

The shadows moved.

Just a faint outline stretching out over the wall, but she shuddered. A blast of cold air passed through her without touching her skin. Her chest and stomach tightened. The form darkened and rose higher, like smoke billowing from a chimney. Stepping to the side, she searched for the best path to stay out of its way. She swallowed and kept her eyes on the opening to the basement stairs.

The lights went out.

A scream burst from her mouth.

"Dammit!" Her dad's feet stomped across the living room floor above her toward the basement. He'd be down in a minute to reset the breaker.

Hurry up.

The power to the house went out at odd times. Sometimes during a storm. Sometimes in the middle of a sunny day. "No rhyme or reason," her dad mumbled often.

Her skin crawled as the cool air moved behind her. She heaved in a deep breath to scream again, but grunted instead as she lurched forward, slamming her feet through anything in her way to the exit.

A metal object clanked against the cement floor as her eyes adjusted to the darkness.

One small basement window provided enough light for her to reach the door leading to the stairs, and she charged up the basement steps just as her dad barreled down past her with a flashlight.

Her dad laughed. "No need to panic. I'll have the lights back on in a second."

Emmie was gasping for breath after reaching the kitchen, and she paused before continuing. "Now I lay me down to sleep," she said. "I pray the Lord my soul to keep. If I should die..." The words soothed her mind.

"Come find me!" Frankie yelled from Mary's section of the house.

"If I should die..." Emmie repeated. "I don't want to die."

The lights surged back to life a moment later, and her dad returned to the kitchen.

"Were you playing down there, kiddo?" He ruffled her hair.

"Yes," she answered. "Didn't you see it?"

"See what?"

"The shadows?"

Her dad gave her a puzzled look. "No. You see something?"

Emmie shrugged. "I guess not."

"Play upstairs for a while."

Emmie nodded. Yes, good idea. Maybe this time it had only been her imagination. She hurried through the living room to the double doors leading into Frankie and his mom's apartment at the back of the house.

She found Frankie's mom washing dishes in a flowery yellow dress. Her long blonde hair was pulled back into a ponytail, and she smiled at Emmie when she glanced over at her. "Well, hello."

"Hi, Mary." Emmie smiled back, watching her rinse off a plate. "Can you play with us?"

"Sorry, but I've got too much to do."

Emmie groaned. *Always too much to do.* But sometimes she'd play with them, and that's when Mary was more like a big sister. So much energy, just like any other kid.

Emmie stared at Mary's face. "You're so pretty. I want to be just like you when I grow up."

Mary paused and frowned at Emmie. "No, you don't, sweetheart. At least wait until finishing high school before having a kid, okay?"

Emmie lost her smile. "Okay."

Mary sighed. "Sorry. Not trying to scare you. What are you playing this time?"

"Hide and seek." Emmie looked around.

"That sounds like fun."

Emmie nodded, then focused again on the game. Frankie was timing her. Was it even worth it to hurry anymore?

She grunted. "Where are you, Frankie?"

She searched behind the recliner chair and ran to Frankie's bedroom. Not in there. She circled around the living room one time before running to the back door. No sign of him in the backyard, but plenty of places to hide out there. She hadn't heard him go outside, but Frankie was good at sneaking around.

"Did Frankie go out?" Emmie asked Mary.

Mary shrugged. "If I told you, that'd spoil the game."

Emmie took that as a yes. She rushed out into the backyard, and the evening sunset cast a warm glow over the landscape. A light breeze rustled the surrounding leaves. She didn't stop to think about which tree he might be hiding behind. Emmie closed her eyes and focused on him. Her Third Eye, the one behind her eyelids, churned with shadows and images as Frankie's form emerged within the darkness. She was getting better at it now, and his shape showed him crouching down behind something. Turning her head with eyes still closed, she pinpointed his location. Up in the air behind the garage. The treehouse.

As her heart beat faster, her smile faded. She remained frozen, even though she knew where to find him.

"I give up," she yelled. "I can't find you."

Maybe if she waited there long enough, Frankie would give up the game and come back on his own.

She opened her eyes. The garage blocked the treehouse and the lower half of the tree. She stared above the garage at the oak's sprawling branches.

She waited for any sign of Frankie.

"Find me!" Frankie's voice called out from behind the garage.

Emmie shook her head and stood still. "No."

"Come find me!" Frankie said again.

"I give up." Maybe Frankie couldn't hear her. She took several steps toward the garage, all the time keeping the bottom half of the tree out of sight. She walked beside the garage, within inches of stepping around the corner. She wouldn't go any further.

"Frankie, I give up."

"You got to find me, Emmie. And guess the card. I'm going to win."

"I don't care. I can't find you."

Frankie laughed. "You're running out of time."

Emmie's legs weakened as her heart raced. *Maybe she won't be there this time.* She clenched her fists. *I'm not afraid.* She would step out in full view of the tree and point at Frankie. That would get him to give up and come down.

She stepped in full view of the tree for the first time in weeks. She glared at it; the branches towered over her.

Its thick base was massive, and her parents had told her the tree had probably stood there for hundreds of years. The one main limb branched off to the side like a giant arm stretching toward the house. Frankie's tree house sat on that arm, but she'd never gone inside it. She never would, no matter how much he begged her.

"Come down now," Emmie said.

Something squeaked against the wood. She followed the wooden steps nailed into the tree up to the trap door in the floor of the treehouse.

"Please come down," Emmie said. "You win. Let's go inside."

A little window along the side of the treehouse opened and Frankie's face appeared. "You're losing really bad this time, Emmie. It's been over three minutes now. You got to come up here and guess the card."

Emmie groaned and took another step forward. She stared at the empty air beneath the tree house. No sign of *her*. Still, Emmie's muscles tensed. It wasn't dark yet, but that hadn't stopped the girl from making a surprise appearance before.

Emmie's eyes widened as she took a few more steps toward the tree. "I'm not going up there."

"How come? You never play with me up here. I'll share it with you. Just climb up."

"I'll wait for you here." She waved for him to come down.

Frankie groaned and climbed out of the house. He dropped to the ground next to the tree and clicked the stopwatch.

"That was just horrible, Emmie. Worst time ever. Five minutes and fifty-seven seconds."

"Okay, let's go inside now." Emmie gestured for Frankie to follow her.

Emmie blinked, and the girl appeared.

She hung from the thick limb holding up Frankie's treehouse. Her head angled off to the side and her tongue hung out as if she were making a funny face. The girl's white nightgown fluttered in the wind, except the air was still now. Her pale face contrasted against the darkened background. The girl's eyes were wide and gazed at Emmie, frozen in a moment of terror. She grinned as if expecting Emmie to laugh.

Not funny. Emmie trembled.

The girl hung only a couple of feet behind Frankie.

"Come here, Frankie." Emmie gestured to him.

"You haven't guessed the card yet."

"Just come over here. I'm done playing. I'm going inside now." Emmie turned her body, but she couldn't look away from Frankie and the girl.

"You're no fun."

Emmie forced herself to look only at Frankie. *Concentrate on Frankie. She'll go away.*

Frankie groaned. "You have to guess the card first."

Emmie forced her legs to walk toward Frankie and the girl. "Just come on."

The girl's grin widened.

Frankie took a step back toward the girl. "You're trying to cheat."

"I'm not. Don't move back!"

Frankie looked around. "Why?"

Emmie lurched forward and grabbed Frankie's hand. She pulled him toward her as the girl lifted herself from the noose and dropped to the ground behind Frankie.

"Hurry." Emmie yanked him forward. "Let's get out of here."

"Ow! You're hurting my wrist."

"Sorry." Emmie winced. Her legs weakened as the girl took a step toward them. Emmie wanted to run inside the house, but she wouldn't let the Hanging Girl terrorize her. That's what her mom and dad had recommended. *"Don't let them terrorize you, honey. Stand up to them. Stand up to your visions. They can't hurt you."*

Maybe they couldn't hurt her, but the fear might kill her.

She towed Frankie along toward the steps to the back door.

Frankie yanked his hand away from her. "Okay, okay. You don't have to be mean about it."

Emmie glanced back at the Hanging Tree. The girl walked behind them, only a few feet away. The girl's face tightened in rage, with her mouth hanging open as if frozen in an eternal scream. Her tongue always hung out to the side. She clawed at Frankie, and her hands passed through him twice. Each time she touched him, Frankie shivered.

"I'm cold," Frankie said.

"Get inside."

Emmie rushed him up the back steps into the house, far from the girl's reach. The door slammed behind them as they jumped inside and crouched down. Emmie caught her breath, and Mary stared at them from the kitchen with a strange look.

"Back so soon?" Mary asked.

"Emmie's afraid of my treehouse," Frankie said.

Emmie didn't argue.

They sat on the floor with their backs against the door. The door rumbled and something thumped on the other side.

"Now I lay me down to sleep, I pray the Lord my soul to keep," Emmie whispered. Her pounding heart slowed. She turned to Frankie. "The Tower."

"What?" he asked.

"The Tower. The card in your pocket. It's number sixteen, The Tower."

Frankie pulled it out. His eyes widened and his mouth dropped open. "How did you do that?"

Emmie shrugged.

❧ 2 ❧

PRESENT DAY

E mmie gathered the items on her desk and put them into the box she'd kept in her car for just such an occasion. It hadn't come as a surprise they were letting her go. Several coworkers had already said their goodbyes to her the previous week, and now it was her turn.

She held up the photo of herself and a friend standing in front of Cinderella's Castle at Disneyland. Good times. At least she had enjoyed a few tourist attractions while she had a chance. She placed the photo in the box with the other knickknacks and glanced around at her coworkers, who were busy doing the same thing.

The woman in the cubicle next to her had three children. Lots of photos on her desk. How would she deal with all the changes? Ray, their supervisor, had given them a heads up about the poor state of the business, but it hadn't done much to lessen the sadness of leaving people she regarded as friends.

She would miss her coworkers, but the job itself had

sucked. Mind-numbingly boring. She had come into the job with all the joy of a teenager in a new relationship, but now it was a dysfunctional mess, and she was looking forward to the divorce.

Assembling corporate reports and prospectuses for financial papers hadn't been her dream job after all. Not by a long shot. She'd studied graphic design for marketing for four years and loved every minute, but this job had sucked the life out of her.

She considered her other options for work. Caricature artist at an amusement park? In five minutes she could draw a portrait of her boss that would have her coworkers roaring with laughter, but doing it full time didn't appeal to her. Lots of other companies around Los Angeles were looking for her skills at design, but they wanted several years of experience. She only had two years of real agency experience, as the first two years out of college doing logo designs and letterheads at a print shop didn't count. Grunt work. Nothing worth putting in her portfolio. Over the last two years she had struggled hard to get a professional portfolio together, but now she was tired and burned out. Time for a break.

Jack, from the row of desks across the room, walked up beside her and scanned her possessions. "What are you going to do now?"

He wasn't the nosy type, but he wasn't one to care either. Probably just wondering if Emmie had any job leads for him since they'd given him the boot, too.

"I can't afford to pay the rent without a job, so... got to go." Emmie packed away a blood-red vase, something she'd picked up in a thrift shop, and some artificial pink roses, trying to maintain a smile at the same time.

"Go where?"

"Minnesota."

"Minnesota? What's back there?"

He had a point. "My parents' old house. I don't want to leave, but I've sent out a hundred resumes over the last few weeks, like everyone else here, and nothing has worked out. I wish I could stay in LA, but I need a job. A good job."

"I hear you." Jack nodded and glanced around at the others packing up their items. "At least you got a place to go to. Have you talked with Ruby yet? Maybe she has a job for you."

"Yes. I already spoke with her. She's got all the help she needs. Nobody's hiring right now with the economy the way it is. It's a shame that I can't stay, but I have no choice."

"Let's do coffee before you leave. Get a few friends together and go to that place down the street one more time."

"Absolutely. I've got your number."

Wendy came up beside Jack. "Emmie, there's a woman outside asking for you."

Emmie looked in the direction of the front desk. "What's her name?"

"She didn't say."

Emmie couldn't see the front window so well, but a moment later the woman pressed her face against the glass. The same woman who'd approached her at the cafe at lunch. God only knows how she'd found out where Emmie worked. Good thing she was on her way out. No more harassment.

"Thank you." Emmie turned and looked down the hall toward the rear exit. "I wonder if I can sneak out the back."

Emmie replayed the conversation she'd had with the woman at lunch. Had she revealed too much? Or maybe the woman had glanced at her open laptop while she worked. That had to be it. Must have seen the company's logo on her desktop background and found her.

Wendy looked concerned. "Should I tell her you're busy?"

"Can you tell her I'm already gone?"

"I think she knows you're here. She was pleading to talk with you. Do you want me to call the police?"

Emmie sighed. "No. It's okay. I'll be up there in a minute."

Wendy walked back to the front desk.

"Some nut stalking you?" Jack stared toward the front desk.

"I hope not."

"She begging for money?"

Emmie shrugged.

"Well, don't be too nice out there or they'll never go away. Give them a little and they come crying back for more. Right?" Jack nudged her shoulder with his elbow and laughed.

"I guess."

Jack stepped away. "Coffee later?"

"Sure."

They always found her. Somehow, someone always found her wherever she went. Thank God none of her coworkers had discovered the details of her past. That would have made things a lot more difficult. Some of them would have supported her, but it was better that they only knew the generic facts. Just the whitewashed, happy, everything's-fine version.

Emmie opened the notepad next to her computer keyboard and read it. A list of items she would need to take care of before making her trip back to Minnesota. She dropped it in the box, along with a surfboard souvenir she'd purchased during an afternoon at Redondo Beach. The last item was a heart-shaped glass dish she had occasionally stocked with chocolate candies, although she usually ate them as fast as she filled the bowl.

It had been a lot of work coordinating the move. Getting the rental company to ship her furniture, getting a change of address with the post office, planning a final get together with friends she might never see again, and reserving hotel rooms for her stops on the long stretch of highway.

She had a few thousand dollars in savings, but moving costs and the trip home would eat most of that. She calculated that after arriving back in Green Hills, she would have less than one thousand dollars to her name. At least she had paid off her aging Toyota Corolla. No car expenses and only a student loan bill and some credit-card bills to manage. Nothing too overwhelming, but living in California was expensive, and now the bottom had dropped out. Time to drive back home and start again.

Waving goodbye to a few other coworkers she had barely known, she took one last look around the expanse of cubicles. Lots of talented people behind those walls.

At the front desk, she received her last check and termination papers from Wendy, the HR person. Her supervisor, tall, balding Neal, was there too.

He shook her hand. "I'll miss working with you, Emmie."

Bullshit. You'll forget my name after I step outside. "Thanks. I'll miss everyone too."

Emmie glanced over at the glass windows looking out toward the street. The woman stood outside, hunched over as if she were about to collapse.

"Is she harassing you?" Wendy asked.

"No. I just met her at the cafe today, and I guess she wants to ask me for help with something."

"Help with what?" Neal asked.

"An accident. She thinks I can help her with it."

"You witnessed an accident?" Wendy asked.

"Something like that."

"Is she okay?"

"I don't think so. I'll take care of it. Bye." Emmie nodded to Wendy and her supervisor.

"Take care, Emmie."

Emmie took a deep breath and stepped toward the door. The woman looked so tired and lost. Would she follow Emmie home if she tried to ignore her?

With her box in her arms, Emmie walked outside. The sunlight warmed and blinded her, but it was refreshing to be out of that cubicle cave.

The woman's face lit up when Emmie came through the door. "Oh, hello! Thank you so much for coming out to see me. I'm so sorry to bother you, Emmie." Her expression changed to sorrow and her eyes watered.

"It's okay." Emmie paused in the harsh sunlight.

"You remember me, right? From the cafe?"

"Yes."

"Can I ask you something about what we discussed? I saw you worked here, so I thought maybe I could ask you one more thing. I'm so sorry for following you here, but I hope you don't mind. Please don't call the police on me or anything."

"I won't."

"Remember I told you about my son? I brought his photo, since you needed something to visualize him. Can you help me find him?" The woman held out a 5" x 7" school photo of a dark-haired boy around eleven years old with a tight-lipped smile and bright eyes. "I would really appreciate your help."

Emmie looked at the picture in the woman's hand but made no motion to take it from her. "I'm sorry. I can't help you. Whatever you've heard about me is not true. I'm so sorry."

Stepping past her, Emmie marched toward the company's parking lot.

"Please help me." The woman stepped along beside her. "Maybe just take his photo and think about it. My number is on the back. I've been through so much, and I've talked to everybody in the world. Nobody has an answer for me. You're my last hope."

Emmie shook her head. She gazed into the woman's eyes—her pain ran deep. "There's nothing I can do to help you. It happened a long time ago, and I'm sure you've heard stories, but I can't help you. I wish I could, but I can't."

The woman dropped the picture of her son into Emmie's box.

"Please take his picture with you. Anything you can do would mean so much to me. I don't mean to bother you, but I don't have any other options."

Emmie stepped back. "Just keep asking the police about it. Maybe they'll find him."

She turned her back on the woman and walked away.

The woman called, "Please call me if you see anything. You're my last hope."

"I'm sorry," Emmie mumbled.

Once more, she glanced back at the woman. Her boy stood next to her, staring up at his mother. His mouth opened and closed in silence, speaking words Emmie might have heard if she moved in closer, but it was too much to handle. All of that was behind her now. Far too painful for anyone to bear. It was better for the woman not to know and not to see her son like that.

How could Emmie explain to that woman what had happened? She didn't want to see the boy ever again, the slash across his throat, and the raw flesh hanging down his neck. How could anybody think a sight like would be helpful?

Better that she didn't know.

$\mathbf{3}$

S arah stood beside the hospital bed and clasped the old man's limp hands. Under normal circumstances, the man would have died weeks earlier; but now the machines had taken over his body, and the only signs of life in his physical shell were quick gasps of air followed by long, drawn-out breaths. The monitors beeped and flashed his vital signs. He might go on like that for days, limping along with only a few hours each day of dazed consciousness.

And then what?

Sarah stared at the tubes connected to his arms and face. So much suffering for so little gain. Why keep him alive at this point? The suffering only drew out the pain. Why not just let him pass on and have peace?

Whether he lived or died, either way wouldn't make any difference to his family. They only visited him once a week, and even then only spent thirty minutes of focused time at his side. They spent most of their visits seeking vending machines and checking their phones. No genuine attempt to have a conversation with him. They were all just waiting for the end. Why make him suffer?

The machines churned and chirped with each breath, each

heartbeat. Still, Sarah did her job. She read the numbers and noted them in her mind to record in her charts when she finished. It didn't look good. The machines would pull him through, but he wasn't recovering.

The man's hand twitched. A random muscle spasm? Maybe somewhere in that darkness he sensed her presence at his side. At least she could help him in some small way by showing a little compassion, some humanity within the impersonal business of a hospital bed.

"I'm right here, Walter." She squeezed his hand again. "I hope it helps."

The corner of his mouth twitched, and then his shoulder. Probably just the cool air or the sound of her voice had triggered a reaction. The man's eyelids didn't move.

Sweet dreams, Walter.

Sarah glanced at the clock. She'd been there for five minutes longer than expected. So many other patients waiting for her help. An endless line of suffering that drained her heart and mind every day.

The passion that had driven her to pursue a career in nursing was long gone, and now she could only do her job out of necessity rather than any sense of a greater good. Not in that stark environment, anyway. The hospital's focus was to keep the patient alive, with little thought about their quality of life. They were a corporation. Not their job. Hospitals wouldn't stay in business for long if all their patients died soon after admitting them. The point was to draw them out for as long as possible, not necessarily to drain their wallets, but hospitals measured their success in survival rates. At some point, all the machines and bother to keep them alive made no sense. *Why drag out their lives long after their flames had extinguished?*

Unlike most of the nurses, Sarah tried to remember the names of the patients during their stay. She tried to learn a little about each one of them, if only to give their faces some humanity.

Most of the nurses avoided attachment. Sarah didn't blame them. So many faces and names flew by in a day—almost pointless to even try. Their schedules created a maddening game of jumping between rooms, between different patients and different levels of suffering. There had to be a better way.

"I wish I could set you free." Sarah squeezed Walter's hand.

The lights flickered overhead, and Walter flinched. His fingers tightened around her wrist, but only for a moment. The subtle grasp intensified before he took in a long, deep breath.

A rush of cool air flowed around her. Her chest tingled as an energy ran down her arm and the hand that held Walter. She felt larger than herself as the energy welling up in her pushed into him.

Then a snap. Like a piece of taffy being stretched and breaking apart, the tension between her and Walter's energy broke away.

The alarms sounded. The machines beeped, alerting her that something had gone wrong.

Nothing had gone wrong. Everything was well for Walter.

"Code Blue," the overhead speakers announced.

Sarah released his hand and waited. Walter's Do Not Resuscitate order prevented her from performing CPR. Despite the order, a flurry of footsteps cascaded into the surrounding room. Everyone had a job to do, and they took their positions around the room to make sure they followed the procedures without fail.

Sarah stared at Walter's face. *No need to hurry, he's at peace now.*

She assisted the other nurses as much as possible, checking the tubes and the man's pulse, but she already knew the outcome. He had passed on.

A second nurse checked his wrist. "No pulse."

The doctor hurried into the room a moment later. Sarah smiled to herself and stepped away as the others did their jobs. After a few minutes, the doctor gave the final call: Walter had passed.

Fly away and be free.

～

SARAH WENT BY THE NURSES' STATION ON HER WAY OUT. SUSAN and Julie stood behind the counter, laughing and whispering like two gossiping schoolgirls.

Susan's face lit up when she met Sarah's gaze. "You'll never guess what we just heard."

Sarah stopped and forced a smile. "What did you hear?"

"You knew that freaky psychic girl in high school, didn't you? The one who found that little boy's body?"

Sarah only needed a moment to remember. "Emmie Fisher."

"She's moving back into town," Julie said.

"Tonight." Susan chuckled.

"That cop, John Ratner, is helping her get set up back in the Hanging House. Can you believe that?"

Sarah shrugged.

Julie continued, "I guess she couldn't handle it out there in the big city. Now she's got nowhere else to go but back into that haunted house. John Ratner is cleaning it up for her, making it all nice and pretty, as if that will help. Can you imagine that? The chief of police is bending over backwards to make her feel at home again. Way more than she deserves after abandoning everything, even her parents. But John always had a soft spot for her. Always thought he had to watch over her like some little lost sheep."

Susan grunted. "I hope that little freak gets what she deserves for coming back here."

"Don't call her freak," Sarah said.

Julie laughed. "Oh, now you're defending her. What were some other names you called her in high school? You teased her more than anybody else."

Sarah glanced down at the floor. "I'm not the same person I was back then."

The things I've seen would melt even the coldest heart.

"Well, maybe you'll change your mind when children disappear around town."

Sarah shook her head. "You're wrong about her. We were all wrong."

Julie chuckled. "Just keep a crucifix handy."

Sarah continued on her way out the back door of the hospital. Getting into her car, she let out a deep breath and paused before turning on the radio.

Her mind was still spinning from all the patients she had helped that day. The one bright spot, Walter, lifted her spirit. Maybe her presence had allowed him to relax enough to move on. At least she could do some good in the world, despite being surrounded by so much heartlessness.

Emmie's back at the Hanging House. Time to make things right.

4

The cloudy night sky reflected the streetlights of Green Hills from miles away as Emmie approached. She doubted the town had grown much beyond the population of 24,000 since she'd left. Far from the bustling, crowded streets of Los Angeles, yet just as overwhelming. The memories trickled back.

Her last visit a few years earlier had been brief. An afternoon at the funeral home and cemetery to say goodbye to her parents after their fatal car accident. Some familiar faces joined her, but most of the funeral was a blur. Besides the tears and the heartache, she didn't remember much. On her way out she'd made a quick detour through the center of town, just for nostalgia, but she'd gone nowhere near her old house, and had never intended to again.

"Oh God, what was I thinking?" Emmie cringed. "This is going to suck so bad."

No other choice. At least John and Mary would be there.

She drove into town, coming in from the west side, and slowed down to the unreasonably slow speed limit of thirty miles per hour. At thirty-five miles per hour, a truck closed in behind her and tailgated for several blocks before turning off.

She wouldn't speed. She couldn't afford to get a ticket.

The main street through town was brightly lit, and the store-fronts looked just as she remembered. Groups of teenagers walked the sidewalks, and she scanned their faces. Nobody she knew. Barlow's Supermarket and the drugstore looked the same. Lots of family-owned businesses, at least on that end of town. The newer section, where several chain restaurants had popped up while she was in high school, was straight ahead on the east side. She passed Jay's Bar & Grill and Rupert's Pizza. She suddenly craved pizza. On her right, Mary and Robert's business, the Sunshine Cafe. Now she craved coffee too, but it was closed.

To her right again, as she passed the road leading to the lake, the streetlights faded off into the distance. Her stomach churned.

Emmie stopped at the main light signal in the middle of town. Another group of three teenage boys and two girls howled with laughter as they crossed in front of her car. That had been her not too long ago. One of the girls met her gaze for a moment. Emmie swallowed and turned her face away. *No need to worry. Too young to remember, anyway.*

Someone honked, and Emmie jumped in her seat. The light had turned green.

She raced ahead and turned left up the street toward her house far too fast. The tires squeaked and the underside of her car slammed against the road.

As she approached a darker street ahead, she slowed down. Her heart beat faster. If someone had offered her a place to stay for free back in Los Angeles at that moment, she would have driven all the way there again without stopping.

Not going to happen, girl. Welcome home.

She made one final turn to the right, down the last street at the edge of town. The dead-end sign on the corner reminded her she was almost there. Only a few houses along that street. One to her left, two on her right, and then her house at the end of the block on the left, sitting all by itself with only a single street-light to illuminate the area.

She spotted a police car parked on the street beside her house.

John.

The sight of his car soothed her mind and lightened her heart, but he couldn't stay all night and watch over her. He'd go home after a while, and then she'd be alone with the place all to herself.

Don't think about it, Em. Just hang in there.

She took a deep breath as she slowed in front of her house.

It was worse than she had imagined. One light beamed out through the living room window, and the porch light showed the broken and weathered fence. If the yard had been an animal's fur, then her animal would have had scurvy. Patches of sickly grass and weeds mixed with puddles of water, and mud covered most of it. Her dad had slaved over that lawn every Saturday afternoon, running his lawn mower in endless circles. All that hard work was gone.

The tree in the front yard where she had played on a rope swing in her youth was sagging and dark. It looked dead. No longer the green symbol of life she remembered. Only some brown leaves and a skeleton of bare limbs remained.

A white fence separating her yard from the neighbor's was overgrown with brush and grass. She had run and played beside that fence so many times, racing back and forth with the neighbor kids. Her mom had planted a rose garden along that fence too, but no sign of her hard work either.

Emmie stared at the front door. When she had left nineteen years earlier, she'd sworn never to go back in there. The arcing half circle above the door resembled an open mouth with teeth jutting down toward everyone who entered.

Was she really going to go in?

The rest of the house was dark. To the left of the front door was the kitchen where her mother had cooked so many meals. For the first time in years, she craved her mother's cooking. Goulash, green bean casserole, tuna and noodles, and her favorite thing to come out of that kitchen: chocolate chip cookies.

Three windows stared out at her from the second floor of the house. Two large dark windows on the right led to her parents' old bedroom, and a smaller window on the left to the bathroom.

Emmie pulled her car into the driveway, and the gravel crunched beneath her tires. She parked and turned off the engine.

"It'll be different this time around," she said to no one. "That's for sure. But you're going to be all right."

She opened her mouth and took in two deep breaths before letting her hands fall from the steering wheel to her lap.

Emmie eyed the living room window. A lavender curtain covered it, and the light revealed someone's outline. Probably John. Hopefully John.

He probably saw you drive in and is wondering why you don't get out of the car.

Emmie hesitated to get out even as John walked out the front door and waved at her. He wore something on his head. A hat? She waved back, but her lights were still on. She doubted he could see her.

She turned off the lights and engine as John walked across the sidewalk to her window. He tapped his knuckles against the glass with a grin. A red and silver cone-shaped party hat sat on his head. It sparkled.

Emmie laughed and rolled down the window instead of opening the door. "What's that for?" She pointed at his hat.

"To celebrate your return home. Mary forced me to wear it." John reached up and adjusted it.

Emmie laughed. "Thanks."

"Aren't you coming in?"

Emmie looked toward the house. "I just can't believe I'm here."

John followed her gaze. "It's not so bad—on the inside, anyway."

"Okay, I guess I traveled all this way. Might as well go inside, right?" Emmie rolled up the window and got out. She stood beside her car, stretching her legs before moving forward. "I don't remember it looking so... bad."

"It definitely needs some love and care, but Mary, Robert, and I will help you with that, I promise."

Emmie glanced around. "Is Mary here? I don't see her car."

"Oh, yeah. I was supposed to tell you—Mary couldn't make it. She said sorry, but she wants you to stop by her house tomorrow morning, if you have time. You remember where she and Robert live, right?"

"The farm in the country."

"That's right. She offered to cook you breakfast if you can make it there before nine a.m. Is that too early for you?"

Emmie smirked. "Not too early. I'll be there."

Her legs ached. Three long days of driving had taken a toll on her health. "My joints are all stiff. I feel like rigor mortis is setting in."

John laughed.

She walked with him up the path to the front door. "I guess I should be grateful to have this place to fall back on during such a shitty time in my life, but I still get the feeling I'm being thrown back into jail. Leaving here when I was eighteen was so liberating."

"I'm sure, but don't sweat it. Living in the big city of Los Angeles toughened you up, right?"

"A little."

John rested his hand on her shoulder for a few seconds. "I'll help you if you run into trouble."

Emmie nodded. "Right. I might call you a lot, so be prepared for that." She looked back at her car. "I guess I should start carrying things inside."

"First, have a look at the place. I'll get your stuff in a sec."

A bird fluttered out from the tree in the front yard and screeched as it flew away. Emmie gave a small cry, holding on to

John's arm, and shuddered. "Oh geez, after all I've seen in my life, a bird just scared the crap out of me."

John chuckled. "Birds can be scary. We had a case once of an owl tearing a man's scalp right off, and who were we going to arrest for that?"

Emmie let out a spooked chuckle.

They arrived at the front door, and she put her hand on the handle. "Well, might as well get this over with."

$\mathbf{\mathscr{E}} \quad \mathbf{\mathit{5}} \quad \mathbf{\mathscr{E}}$

E mmie crossed the threshold, and all the memories of the past flooded her. The hardwood floors creaked beneath her feet, just as they had when she'd left seven years earlier. The familiar scent of wood and stale air in the entry passed around her before another smell drowned out everything else—fresh paint.

A banner hung over the kitchen doorway. "Welcome Home, Emmie." Dozens of balloons and colored streamers dangled from the ceiling and walls. All the feel of a child's birthday party. An ugly, blue-shaded lamp in the living room lit the area.

"Notice anything different?" John asked.

Emmie nodded. The gaudy wallpaper her mom had put up so long ago was now gone. They had painted the walls a neutral beige. Horrible as it had been, she immediately missed the old wallpaper.

John ran his hand across a freshly painted wall. "We're not finished yet. Do you like it?"

Not his fault. He's just trying to help.

"Yes," she lied. "Better."

Now she could see that the blue and red cone-shaped hat on

John's head read, "Congratulations!" The cheap banding holding it on his head carved a deep valley across his throat.

She pointed to it. "Are you comfortable in that thing?"

He winced and removed it. "Not really. I think my wife got the child size by mistake."

Emmie chuckled. "How is Claire doing?"

"Much better now that the kids have left for college." He smirked. "You'll see her again one of these days. So busy now with her social work."

The warm smile on John's face contrasted with the expression most law enforcement officers wore, according to her experience. Her mood lifted. She'd rarely seen him without his uniform on, either. With his thick-rimmed glasses, orange and white flannel shirt, and dark khaki pants, he could pass for a high school physical education teacher. His white sneakers looked brand new.

Little patches of gray were mixed with his dark brown hair. He was a few years older than her parents, but she could never consider him to be old. He'd taken care of himself over the years. His muscular, burly physique filled out his shirt, as if he'd just gotten out of the US Marines. His presence gave her courage.

Emmie walked into the kitchen, and John followed her. The linoleum floors revealed well-worn paths to all the most active areas—the kitchen sink to the right, where her mom had slaved over piles of dishes, and the aging refrigerator; the main counter to the left, looking out over the front yard. All the appliances were still there, thank God, since the house went up for sale after the death of her parents. The magnets and photos that had covered the refrigerator door, however, were gone.

Truman Capote's *In Cold Blood* lay cover up on the counter. John walked over and closed it, pushing it to the side as if she'd caught him indulging in candy before supper.

"You still read those mystery books?" Emmie gestured to it.

"All the time. Can't get enough."

"You must have read them all by now...?"

"Not yet."

It was her home, but now stripped of memories. Just a shell of the life she'd left behind.

A small cake of pink and white frosting topped with a single candle sat on the counter.

"I couldn't remember your age," John said, "so I started over, just to be safe."

Emmie chuckled. "Good call."

The door leading down to the basement was cracked open a few inches. A thick darkness lay beyond it. She had never intended to go down there again, but now a heaviness passed through her.

"Do you know if anyone fixed the electrical problems?" Emmie asked.

"I've had an electrician out here twice, but the lights still flicker." John swallowed. "Makes everyone think it's haunted."

Emmie forced a grin. "It's okay. I'll deal with it."

She closed the door and walked back into the living room. Her parents' beat-up, three-cushion brown couch sat in the same spot it had always been, but her dad's matching recliner was gone, the spot where he'd spent so many hours watching TV. She missed the shelves crowded with family portraits and an antique rocking chair that had sat in the corner. All her mom's personal touches had been stripped away. Only memories remained.

Her mom used to work at a massive wooden desk against a back wall that had held shelves of knickknacks and souvenirs. She'd used that desk for business: paying the bills, writing letters, working on her computer. Her other desk had been upstairs in the extra bedroom where she could be alone to focus on her "hobby."

"As you can see," John gestured to the couch, "we spared no expense to make you feel at home." He smirked and attempted to cover a large gash in a cushion sewed up with duct tape. It was kind of gnarly, but she wouldn't say so.

A loud crack filled the air. John ducked as Emmie froze. A

piece of shredded red latex dropped to the floor beside the couch.

"Holy shit," John said. "Cheap-ass balloons. They don't make them like they used to."

Emmie laughed.

"Everything in the house is either leftover from the auction or from Mary or me. We pitched in to make sure you'd be comfortable." John gestured to a small TV on a wooden stand beneath the main window. "I wasn't sure if you'd have one or not, so I went ahead and installed rabbit ears on this little baby. I think you can get the over-the-air channels until you get your cable installed."

"Thanks."

"We found some of your mom's dishes in the garage, and some kitchen items."

"I don't need much. I shipped several boxes of stuff, whatever I couldn't fit in my car. Hopefully it arrives by Monday. How much stuff is left over from the auction?"

"Lots. Your mom had a lot of *unique* items." He raised his eyebrows wryly. "Strange that the Ouija boards didn't sell."

"Is it all in the garage?"

"Most of it. Dozens of plastic totes. Plenty to sort through when you have the time."

Emmie stepped over to the stairs, going up to the bedrooms. The hall light was on, but she paused.

"Your bedroom is all ready for you," John said in an encouraging way.

Emmie stared up into the window at the top of the stairs. The blinds were open.

"Something wrong?" John asked.

"No." Emmie took another deep breath. "I'll get used to it. It's just a little freaky being in here without my mom and dad around. It doesn't feel the same."

"I understand. You just need to make it your own."

Emmie walked upstairs, her footsteps echoing through the empty hallways.

"I'll just wait down here," John said from the living room.

"All right."

She closed the blinds when she reached the top and glanced into the bathroom on her left. No more arguments over who would use it first. She circled around the railing to the right, toward the bedrooms. Her parents' bedroom was the first door on the right. It was shut, and she left it that way. Too many memories inside.

The next door on her right was the extra bedroom that her mom had used as a reading library. Her *hobby* room.

Emmie's chest tightened and her face warmed as she glanced inside. The smell of old books hung in the air, yet it was empty. Just a dusty floor now, but she remembered everything—her mom's cluttered desk void of family pictures, walls adorned with occult symbols, stacks of books and magazines. An antique crimson leather chair had sat in the corner, surrounded by shelves full of books that her mom had collected over the years. Maybe if she hadn't been reading all the time, she could have done something about the bigger issues in Emmie's life. More important issues, like protecting her from the Hanging Girl.

Emmie looked to the center of the room and sneered. All the hours she'd sat respectfully listening to her mom lecture about her *gift*.

So important and unique and beautiful.

"You really called this shit beautiful, didn't you, Mom? What the hell were you thinking?"

She clenched her teeth and slammed the door.

"You okay up there?" John called from downstairs.

"For the most part," she answered.

Emmie continued. A little further down the hallway was a small door, as if built just for a child. It led into the attic, and she had played in that room with Frankie a lot, at first. A perfect playhouse, except for the occasional spider and the chilly air in the winter, until the Hanging Girl had found her in there. After that, never again.

Straight ahead at the end of the hall was her old bedroom. The door was closed, but she opened it and walked in without pausing. Everything was ready for her, just like John had said. A queen-size mattress pushed up against the wall, covered by a thick, flowery comforter. The dresser they'd brought was old, and it would work just fine. She wasn't picky. But the blackness of the window looking out over the backyard caught her eye. The blinds were open.

Even though she couldn't see anything beyond her own reflection in the glass, she stepped forward and snapped them shut. It wouldn't make any difference, anyway. The Hanging Girl would know she was back.

Emmie left the room and returned downstairs. She faced the door on the left that led into Mary's old apartment.

"We haven't done anything in there yet," John said.

"I don't blame her for not tackling it."

Before she could talk herself out of it, Emmie walked to the door and opened it. She opened the second door, the one that her mom and dad had explained was for Mary's privacy, and flipped on the lights. At her feet was the trapdoor down to the basement where Mary had needed to go for a bath or a shower. Only a sink and a toilet in her apartment. A poor arrangement for her, but that was how someone had built the house.

John came to stand beside her. "We didn't go into the basement yet either. Still, lots of work that could be done to fix this place." After a pause, he added, "Don't let it get you down. You're not alone in this."

"I appreciate it."

Two large windows faced the backyard, although there the blinds were mercifully closed. Two bedrooms on the right. The first one had been Mary's and the second one in the corner had been Frankie's. Both doors were closed.

Emmie stared at the door handle to Frankie's room. The

words simply came out because they had to: "I miss him. My first best friend." *And my last.*

"He was a good kid," John said. "Every time I go by the lake, I remember the spot where he drowned."

Emmie nodded. "The place where I found him."

6

"See you again Saturday." John opened the door and looked back. "A few more days and you won't recognize this place anymore."

"Promise?"

"Don't worry about a thing." John nodded and walked away.

Emmie watched him go, waving as his police car drove away. It wasn't so bad until his lights vanished from sight. The dark surrounded her then, with only one streetlamp half a block away to keep total night from swallowing her.

Just her and the house now.

Closing and locking the door, she flipped off the porch light, then turned back into the living room to get ready for bed.

She stopped. A gaping blackness filled the doorway leading into Mary's apartment. She'd left the doors wide open.

Her heart beat faster, but she walked over without pausing. Too damn tired to be scared. She closed and locked both doors.

She stared at the door handle.

What did you expect would happen? She's gone. Enough.

She walked back across the living room toward the stairs. If she had Internet, she could take her mind off her loneliness by watching mindless videos or reading social media. Without that, her imagination was free to run wild in the emptiness of the house.

At least no sign of *her* yet.

She was too exhausted from the long drive to worry. Whatever happened would happen. She would deal with it, as always.

Earlier that morning she'd been in Nebraska checking out of her hotel room and preparing for the final stretch of highway back to Minnesota. Now, twelve grueling hours later, she'd arrived in the last place she wished to be. Her body cried out for sleep, and she couldn't argue.

She trudged upstairs, passing her mom and dad's empty bedroom. The echoes of the hollow house reminded her of her loneliness. Maybe it was time to get a pet. Maybe a dog, or just a cat.

Not this conversation again.

Can't do it. A pet meant responsibilities and made travel more difficult. *Maybe later, after I settle down. But one thing is for sure—it* absolutely *won't be here. Got to stay mobile.*

Once her bedroom door was shut, she changed into her pajamas and sat on the edge of the bed. For a moment, just a moment, she felt as though her mom was sitting next to her.

Her mom's warm, yet firm voice played in her mind like a recording she couldn't switch off. "Meditate and communicate."

"Nope." Emmie stared at the floor. "Not anymore, Mom."

She snapped back to reality, climbed into bed and buried herself beneath the sheets. The bed John and Mary had prepared was perfect. Clean sheets were always soothing.

Meditate and communicate.

"Leave me alone." She closed her eyes for a second, before something thumped downstairs.

Her breath paused.

Plumbing. Just those old damn pipes. She would get some earplugs the next day.

She nudged lower below the sheets and her eyes cracked

open again. Another soft thump downstairs. Sounded like it was coming from inside the walls. *Had* to be the plumbing.

The moonlight's glow peeked through the window shades, allowing in enough light for her to see everything clearly.

Something creaked farther down the hallway.

Just the house settling. Forever settling. Lots of creaks in an old, neglected house.

Had anyone repaired anything since her parents' death?

She closed her eyes again and drifted off until something fluttered against her window screen. The wood creaked around the window's frame. The wind was picking up, and she hoped it would rain soon. A *real* Midwest thunderstorm would be nice— one that shook the house. No real thunderstorms in Los Angeles. She missed the drama and excitement of Minnesota lightning crashes.

Something creaked and knocked against wood down the hallway, like a door closing. The room cooled. A gust of wind blew harder against her window.

Just some leaks. Another thing to fix.

One solid thump came from the stairway. Once more, her heart sped up.

Just an old house. Definitely get that fixed tomorrow.

Another one and then another. The sounds changed tone as they continued. Footsteps up the stairs. No, impossible.

If she weren't so tired, she would get up and explore the cause. The Hanging Girl was gone. She couldn't *still* be there.

The footsteps continued. Soft, thoughtful steps, like someone creeping toward her. Maybe someone had broken into the house and been hiding out.

A burglar, if she were lucky. She nervously smiled. They wouldn't find anything of value in her house.

More footsteps along the hallway. Definitely approaching. They'd be at her bedroom door soon.

Emmie pulled the sheet up over her face and groaned. It can't be her.

Why not? Do you think she just magically went away? Disappeared into the ether? Maybe she was just waiting all this time, in case you came back home. Hanging out—no pun intended—and planning for the day if you ever dared to walk back through that front door again.

You abandoned the house, Emmie. You ran away and gave it to her, and now she's angry you're back. She wants your attention. Not just attention—the girl wants to harm you, to hang you in that tree, so you join her in the afterlife.

Emmie's hot breath warmed her face under the sheets as her heart kept drumming. *How dare that girl come back into my house again, after all I've been through?*

Maybe it's not her.

Who else could it be?

A burglar. Please, God, let it be a burglar.

Her bedroom latch clicked, and the door squeaked open.

Emmie's skin chilled. Her mind jumped between thinking of a way to protect herself, but also focusing on a better explanation. She pulled up a random mental image of driving across the desert. A good, relaxing image. The expanse of landscape around her and the calm sun sliding through her car windows.

Her floor squeaked fast and high, and then low and slow. Weight shifting.

"Go away," Emmie said beneath the sheets. "I'm done with you."

The floor squeaked again, and something bumped against the side of her bed. Emmie shuddered. The girl had never touched her or anything around her physically before. Maybe it *was* an intruder. She had no protection at all. Her mind raced back to a self-defense class she had taken as a teenager. She'd learned how to flip over and disarm an attacker, and how to escape from an assault. Too tired to fight back. No way to get out now.

Something touched her foot and pulled on the sheet covering her.

Emmie kicked the blanket. "Get out of here or I'll call the police."

Her foot hit only air, and the floor squeaked again.

She clutched the sheet tighter, forming fists as she prepared to fight back.

"Now I lay me down to sleep, I pray the Lord my soul to keep," she whispered between gasps of breath.

She was cowering like a little kid. But what was she supposed to do? She was powerless.

It could only be the girl or an intruder. If she weren't so tired, she could handle the situation better, but her mind wasn't clear.

Through the thin fabric an outline appeared, a vague silhouette of a figure standing over her against the ambient light in the room. The figure moved closer, hovering above her face, only inches away. Emmie stared into the place where the figure's eyes would be. It had to be the girl. An intruder wouldn't have waited so long to attack her. But the girl had touched the bed, or had that been from her own muscles twitching?

Emmie pushed her face back into her pillow as far as she could. She repeated the nursery rhyme louder and louder, over and over.

Her breath was like a furnace beneath the sheet.

I'm going to face you now. On three.

One... Two... Three!

She punched forward at the figure's face with her eyes closed. She screamed and kicked, lurching up into a sitting position and throwing the sheet to the side as her eyes adjusted to the darkness.

"Get the hell out of here!" She jumped to her feet and wobbled.

Nobody there. She kicked at the darkness under her bed. Maybe the figure had dropped and hid under there.

Her pulse pounded as she switched on a small lamp and checked under her bed again. Nothing. She scanned the room with her fists clenched and whipped open the closet door, ready to pound at the intruder. Nobody.

The bedroom door was now open. She stared down the hallway.

"Welcome home, Em." She walked over and shut her door. Too tired to chase them.

She returned to her bed and sat on the corner, gasping and running her fingers through her hair. She screamed, "Meditate and communicate, my ass!"

7

Of all the days Emmie had lived in Green Hills, that morning struck her as especially beautiful. Maybe it was the flowers in bloom in the garden as she pulled into the driveway of Mary and Robert's farm, but the place radiated the feeling of the perfect home: a two-story white house with a big old-fashioned porch. Seclusion—no neighbors in sight. Open fields on one side and a pine forest on the other.

Not a large farm; just a small red barn and a handful of cows grazing in the pasture, but plenty to handle for a middle-aged couple without children. Mary had often talked about moving to the country, and she finally got what she wanted.

Emmie climbed out of her car and walked up the sidewalk to the front door. During her last visit to Green Hills for her parents' funeral, she'd only visited with Mary at the funeral for a few hours, but everything had been so dark during that time. She hadn't wanted to be in town any longer than necessary. Thank God Mary had offered to take care of the auction so she wasn't forced to enter the house again. Aside from family photos, she'd never wanted to see any of it again.

Rows of flowers lined the edge of the house, and the double garage was open, revealing a large tool bench along the back wall.

A giant Old West wagon wheel was propped up against the house, surrounded by a flowerbed. Must be something Robert owned. He was the cowboy type, in blue jeans and boots most of the time, with tight-fitting button-down shirts and a large silver belt buckle to complete the look.

Emmie reached the door and knocked. Someone rustled inside, and a moment later Mary's face appeared within the darkness of the frosted glass window in the door. She opened it and her face lit up. "Oh, my goodness, Emmie!"

"Hi, Mary." Emmie stretched out her arms, and they hugged. She'd forgotten how wonderful it felt to have someone who cared about her embrace her. Mary's familiar flowery perfume took her mind back to her childhood. "You look younger than ever."

Mary backed away and laughed, gesturing to her turquoise blouse and white shorts. "Pretty good for a forty-something, huh? A happy marriage will do that to you."

Mary's long blonde hair was cut shoulder length now. Her bright blue eyes beamed behind thin pink glasses.

Emmie gestured to the pasture. "I saw the cows."

Mary laughed. "More trouble than they're worth. Robert's always out in the barn with them or working at the cafe. I'm not much of a cowgirl." She motioned toward the house. "This is my domain. I mostly just watch the castle and reap all the rewards."

Mary led her inside with her arm still around Emmie's back.

The delicious scent of coffee caught Emmie's attention. "It's been so long. I can't wait to get caught up on everything."

Just inside the door were some older photos of Mary and Frankie. Emmie's smile faded at seeing Frankie's sweet face. Her heart ached. It was a school portrait, with Frankie's straight hair matted down and slicked over to the side. His large, thick glasses reminded her of his intelligence, and his wide, contagious smile of his energy. That boy had always been on the run. Not an ounce of patience in him.

But now, after almost twenty years, it was a boy she barely

knew. She wasn't the same person either. So much had changed, and yet she was forever linked to him.

Emmie stared into his eyes for a few more seconds and then followed Mary into the kitchen.

"Make yourself at home," Mary said. "Would you like anything to drink?"

"Coffee? I can smell it."

Mary grinned. "My specialty. What's your favorite?" She motioned to an assortment of small, flavored cups next to the coffee maker.

"I'll take the French Vanilla."

"Iced?"

"That would be awesome."

"Got it. Have a seat." Mary gestured to the kitchen table and went to the counter to make the coffee.

Emmie sat and glanced around the living room. More photos filled the walls, this time family portraits of Robert and Mary together, without Frankie—some of them wedding pictures and vacation photos of mountains and streams. The outdoors. Mary had always talked about building a log cabin in the mountains. It was obvious she had traveled a lot since Emmie had left town.

Another picture of Frankie caught Emmie's eye. He stared directly into the camera this time, and something about the way he looked at that moment brought back a flash of Frankie standing at the edge of the lake. Maybe a time they had gone swimming together?

One framed photo showed Robert riding alone on a gondola through the canals of Venice, Italy. A wide grin stretched across his face. An odd place for him to vacation.

"I forgot that Robert traveled to Europe." Emmie studied his face. So much younger and maybe the only photo of him smiling.

"Yes, after Maggie divorced him, he went there with his brother. Tough time for him back then."

"I didn't think he traveled much."

"No, not much."

Dishes clanked in the kitchen. Mary cleared her throat. "When John told me you were coming back, I just knew I had to do something special for you. Did you like what we did to the house?"

"It was wonderful, yes."

"I'm so sorry I couldn't make it last night. The cows broke out of their pasture right before you arrived. Something must've spooked them pretty good to break out the way they did—crashed through the gate. We had no choice but to take care of it right away. Nothing like chasing down cattle in the middle of the night."

"I guess you're taking this farming thing seriously."

"Well, like I said, I'm no cowgirl, but I had to learn the ropes, so to speak. For Robert."

The coffee machine stopped gurgling, and Mary brought the cup to the table.

Emmie sniffed at it and grinned. "Aren't you going to have a coffee?"

"I've got another surprise in store." Mary went to the refrigerator and dug around inside. "I always seem to be working in the kitchen lately, either at the cafe or at home."

"How did you come up with the idea of a cafe?"

"It was Robert's idea. I told him I wanted to change careers after we got married. I was so fed up with the school administration grind. So he saw that place was for sale and we bought it. Simple as that. He thought it would help keep my mind off... you know." Mary dug out two eggs from the refrigerator and brought them over to a large bowl on the counter. "You know what I'm going to make, don't you?"

Emmie smirked. "Are you really going to bake cookies after all these years?"

"Why not? You love them. You do still love them, right? I'm sure you haven't lost your sweet tooth."

"I still love them, I just can't eat a dozen anymore."

"That's okay. Eat whatever you want. You can take the rest home with you."

Mary mixed the flour and sugar and added the butter.

"It smells good already."

"You just wait. These are even better than the cookies in the cafe. These are the real homemade ones." Mary laughed. "I used to make you and Frankie batches of cookies all the time. Do you remember that?"

"How could I forget?"

"You two would have the whole tray eaten within an hour. I wasn't so happy about it then, but looking back it's hilarious. He would eat the whole batch and not even have an upset stomach. Kids are like that, I guess. All that running around and screaming. They burn a lot of calories so fast."

"Frankie had all the energy, just like his father," Mary said softly. "I just spent my time trying to keep up with him."

Mary had moved to Green Hills with Frankie's father after she got pregnant. A teen still, she had quit high school, left home against her parents' wishes, and followed her boyfriend to a small town because he was promised a great job there that never panned out. Once she gave birth to Frankie, it wasn't long before he abandoned them.

Instead of moving back to the city, she had stayed in town, gotten a job at the local high school in the administration department, and appeared at the house to apply for the apartment at the back.

But Emmie said nothing about Frankie's father. She knew the story, but no one had ever really talked about it to Mary. She'd often heard her mother and father whisper, "Poor Mary, so young —and so lonely."

Emmie didn't even remember Mary having a boyfriend, till she upped and married Robert. Good for her. Good for both.

She watched Mary's face to gauge whether she was thinking of that time, or of Frankie's death. She could still hear her cries when she was told by John the little boy had been found, drowned. Mary must still blame herself for not knowing he was swimming in the lake unsupervised, even after being told never to do it.

Without a reaction, Mary continued adding ingredients. After a moment, she said, "Robert pulled me through those times. Only a person who has lost a child can understand what it's like. And sometimes two parents who lose a child together grieve differently and drift apart." She threw Emmie a look. "I would never say it was lucky for me that his wife left him after they lost their son. That's too horrible, and he tried so hard to make her happy. But she did leave, and we found each other. And he helped me survive."

Without waiting for Emmie to reply, Mary finished putting the cookie dough into the oven, dropped the oven mitts on the counter, and gestured toward the living room. "Let's go sit on the couch. A little more comfortable."

Several antique weapons hung against one wall, between framed photos of scarlet sunsets and wildlife: daggers, swords, a rusty revolver, and an old musket with a menacing bayonet perched at the tip.

"Does that musket still work?"

"Heavens, no. Robert keeps all his guns locked up."

A small, rectangular wooden display on the wall held a dozen colorful Murano marbles.

"Frankie's marbles," Emmie said.

"What's that?"

"I like how you displayed Frankie's old marble collection."

"Beautiful, aren't they? Most of them are gone now. Robert gathered the rest and built the display for me."

Another photo of Frankie sat on the coffee table next to the couch. The shadows overhead blackened Frankie's eyes, but his mouth was a little open, as if he'd been caught in the middle of a laugh.

"Oh," Mary said, "I'm so sorry. I forgot that Frankie is everywhere in this house. Does that bother you?"

"No, it's okay. Of course, I miss him even after all these years."

Mary's eyes watered. "It's funny, I walk by those pictures of Frankie every day, and instead of sadness it reminds me of how wonderful it was to spend those years with him. I never want to forget his smile. He was such a sweet boy."

Emmie swallowed before she caressed Mary's hand and said, "It's going to take me a while to get used to living back here again, but you and John already helped me feel better about everything."

"Well, I hope you never leave." She held on to Emmie's fingers. "You know, having you and Frankie playing every day in the apartment those years was like having two children. So after he was gone, you helped me to believe I still had one child left. I don't know how else to describe it. Maybe someday, if you have kids, you'll understand."

Emmie chuckled. "Before I can have kids, I need to get a boyfriend."

"You didn't leave behind some heartbroken young man when you moved back here? I can't believe it." Mary laughed. "You keep smiling like that, and a thousand gorgeous guys will beg you to marry them."

A little later, the timer on the oven dinged, and Mary took out the first pan of cookies. She put in the second batch and stood by the oven. "Robert should be home soon. He takes care of the morning rush at the cafe, and I handle the rest of the day. It works out."

"I'm sure I'll stop by there often for coffee."

Mary beamed. "I'd like that. The town itself hasn't changed all that much since you left. That reminds me—Pastor Wallace says hi, although you probably shouldn't make too much of that. He's just being friendly, as usual."

"I don't think he ever liked me, or my parents. Because of all that stuff we were into. Big bad evil tarot cards." Emmie imitated a monster for a moment and then laughed.

"You left an impression on him. He's not such a bad guy, but he definitely has a strong opinion about all the nighttime excursions to the cemetery and the publicity. He didn't want this town to become famous for the wrong reasons, and I don't blame him at all. Green Hills shouldn't be a circus, you know?"

Emmie nodded. "I understand. It was a stressful time."

"Have you talked with any of your high school friends?"

"No. I didn't have many friends, anyway. There was Olivia, do you remember her? I used to sleep at her house when her mom would work all night and we could have beer. Sometimes parties." She laughed at Mary's face of exaggerated shock. "And then there were a couple of girls I've kept in touch with through social media, but they're not here anymore."

"I know, most young people leave, like you. Not enough excitement."

"I've actually only seen John so far." Emmie let the silence lengthen as she took a sip of cold coffee. "I'm not sure how people will react to me. Like you say, no excitement, so they'll remember I found Frankie, and no one knows how. Not even me." She laughed. "I'm sure they think it's strange we're friends."

Shaking her head, Mary looked deep into her eyes. "That's nonsense, Emmie. I'm forever grateful to you, and your friendship is the most important thing in my life. Well, in addition to Robert's love. What do these people have to do with any of it? Do they think it would have been better for me not to know? Not to find my Frankie?"

"But they thought—"

Mary squeezed her fingers harder. "I don't care what they thought. I care about what I was feeling." Mary's gaze jumped from Emmie's face to her fingers, then she relaxed her grip and leaned back. "Sorry. They looked at us funny too, when Robert and I were married so soon after Frankie's death, but I dealt with the tragedy as best I could and found the help I needed. Some people in this town just don't want to understand that. So keep your head up high, Emmie, and to hell with them."

"I'll try." Emmie nodded, attempting a smile.

Mary leaned toward her. "Maybe I shouldn't ask this right now, but have you had any... you know, *feelings* lately?"

Emmie lost her grin and shook her head. "I don't really experience that stuff anymore. I think it was just a phase in my life. Or, in Frankie's case, a miracle."

"Yes, definitely a miracle for me. Such an... amazing gift."

"I would gladly have given that gift away if I'd had the choice. But it's gone now, and I don't ever want to deal with it again."

Mary smiled sympathetically. "Yes, that's probably best." Her gaze locked on something over Emmie's shoulder, and her face brightened. "Robert's here, finally. Let me check on those cookies."

Mary stood up as Robert walked in the door, and Emmie joined her in the kitchen.

Robert was never the social type. A muscular, burly man with a permanent scowl on his face and always wearing a baseball cap, he had a scruffy beard and a menacing stare. It was difficult to tell if he hated you or just the world. He glanced at Emmie as he walked in, then broke into a warm smile as he approached Mary and kissed her on the cheek.

"Busy this morning?" Mary asked.

"Always busy." He turned to Emmie. "Mary said you were moving back. You must've forgotten the winters are brutal here. Won't be long before it starts snowing. You sure you want to run away from that warm California sunshine?"

"Not really, but I ran out of money."

Robert nodded. "What'll you do back here?"

"I'm not sure yet. I can do some freelance projects to pay the bills, but at least I won't have a mortgage payment."

"That's a big house to take care of for just one person."

"I can handle it."

Mary gathered the first batch of cookies together and put them into a sealed plastic container. She held it out toward

Emmie. "I should probably get going to work now. This should help you feel better for a day or two."

Emmie laughed and reached for it. "Maybe only a few hours."

Mary leaned in and whispered, "And please let me know if you have any more feelings about—"

Something crashed against one of the living room windows. Emmie started, and Mary dropped the container of cookies to the floor.

"Good God," Robert yelled as he stormed out the door. "What the hell was that?"

A gooey red mess streaked down the glass.

Emmie's stomach churned. She followed Mary outside and around the house to where Robert stood over the mangled, bloody body of a crow. Its wings fluttered and twitched as it struggled to fly away.

"Well, might as well put it out of its misery." John grabbed its head, and before Emmie could look away, he spun the body in a circle. Something cracked beneath the feathers, and the crow stopped moving.

Emmie lost her appetite.

❧ 8 ❧

The narrow strips of wallpaper in the living room tore off easily, although not completely. Emmie pulled at them with one hand as she bit into a peanut butter and jelly sandwich she'd slapped together a few minutes earlier. She moved along to the back wall that separated the main section of the house from Mary's old apartment.

Ripping the paper from the wall satisfied her on a deep level, as did tossing each piece into the air without a thought about cleaning up the mess. She grinned as she tore faster and began to claw the rest away.

Of course, she hadn't gone out anywhere—not even to get groceries, though the food John and Mary had left for her would soon run out. The town wouldn't have forgotten about Frankie's death, and she cringed at the thought of being stared at again. It didn't matter she was a grownup now—they would point and still suspect her of witchcraft or murder. Still, nothing she could do about it, except fix up the house as fast as she could with what-ever little money she had left and just sell it. There had to be *someone* out there who wanted to buy an aging haunted house at the edge of town.

A knock at the door made her jump.

Oh, great.

Emmie crept to the window and peeked out. A white minivan sat in the driveway. Not Mary or John. She could pretend she wasn't home, but her car was in the driveway.

She went to the door and paused.

Please be a salesman or a Jehovah's Witness or a neighbor kid wanting me to buy some overpriced candy for the school fundraiser. Whoever it is, I'll be polite. Promise. I'll tell them to... politely... get the hell off my property. With a smile.

Emmie opened the door.

A familiar face stood staring at her, although she couldn't remember the young woman's name. She had tinted purple hair and a wide grin.

"Hi Emmie," she said. "Do you remember me?"

Samantha? Susan? Emmie searched her memories.

A potted plant in the girl's hands caught Emmie's eye. Maybe she would throw it at her and run away. Emmie glanced around. Was somebody pranking her?

"I..." Emmie narrowed her eyes.

"You don't remember me. I don't blame you. I'm Sarah Swanson; we went to school together." She ran her fingers through her hair. "My hair wasn't purple back then."

Emmie remembered a little more. "Yes, I do recall you from my class. You have an older sister, right? For some reason, I was thinking you were your sister." Emmie laughed. "I was wondering why she was here."

"That's okay. I look a lot like her. I'm sure I look older now. Just stopped by to say hi and bring you this housewarming gift." Sarah held out the plant.

Emmie accepted it. "Oh, geez. Thank you very much. Not too many people dare to stop by this house."

Sarah shrugged. "I'm not worried. So, I know this is kind of odd, but the reason I stopped by is so I can talk with you, if that's okay?"

"What about?"

"Well, I'm a nurse now and—you can tell me to go away if you want, I don't blame you—but I've dealt with people who die occasionally..."

"You want me to contact spirits for you."

"No, no, nothing like that. I'm just hoping I could talk with you about some things I've experienced. Things you might help me understand, since you'd know about them better than anyone."

Emmie glanced out at the street again. No signs of a setup. "I'm not sure I'll be any help." She opened the door further and Sarah stepped inside. "You want something to drink?"

"Maybe just water. Thank you." Sarah glanced around the living room. "I've heard so much about this house."

"Not much to see." Emmie carried the plant over to her card table and set it down beside her laptop. "Thanks for the plant. I like it very much. I should get some flowers to liven up this place. As you can see, there's plenty of space to fill."

"Everything's gone, huh?"

"Almost everything." Emmie went into the kitchen and filled two glasses with ice and water. She came back and handed one to Sarah, who sipped it. "We didn't talk much in high school, did we?"

Sarah lowered her glass, gulping the water, and looked guilty for a second. "Not too much. I'm sorry about that."

"That's all right. Most people avoided me. Long time ago."

At least Sarah was being friendly. Emmie motioned toward the only place to sit and talk, the old sofa. Each of them took a seat at a different end. Sarah looked around for a moment, then set her purse and glass of water on the floor at her feet. No small tables nearby, but at least it was clean.

"You said you were a nurse?" Emmie asked. Whatever Sarah wanted, might as well get it out in the open.

Sarah nodded. "At a hospital in Minneapolis. It's a demanding job, that's for sure. I used to love it, but now I'm not so sure."

"You drove out here all the way from Minneapolis?"

"No. I live in Larston Lake. I carpool back and forth. It works out, especially in the wintertime when the roads are so bad. I suppose you remember what that's like."

"Yeah. I'm not looking forward to the winter here at all. I'm sure when January comes, I'll really miss the California sunshine." Emmie drank some water. "How did you know I was back?"

"Oh, word gets around. Do you remember Susan Johnson? I work with her too."

Emmie sneered. "Yes."

Sarah chuckled. "You *do* remember her."

"Hard to believe she's a nurse. I never would've guessed she had an ounce of compassion in her."

"That's her. Yeah, she was rough around the edges back then, and she hasn't changed much, but I guess that's what it takes to be an effective nurse dealing with some of those patients."

"She bullied me in high school."

Sarah lost her smile. "I saw that, and maybe you don't remember, but I was part of that crowd too. I'm sorry. I think we were all a little scared of you after you found Franklin's body and all the rumors circulated about what you could do. Everyone fears death and spirits and all that. We were just kids."

"I guess. It still hurt." Emmie also put her glass down and looked into Sarah's eyes. "So, what did you want to talk about?"

"I guess I should just say it." Sarah cleared her throat. "Like I said, as a nurse I come into contact with many people who are sick and dying, and I'm wondering if you can help me explain something." She struggled for words before adding, "This is going to sound really weird, but I experience something *profound* right before a patient dies."

Emmie scoffed. "Trust me, nothing's weird after all the shit I've seen in my life. What do you mean by profound, though? Something spiritual?"

"When I go to a patient who I think is suffering a lot, need-less suffering, I stand by their bedside and meditate." Sarah tilted her head and looked at the floor. "In my mind, I surround them with a warm light because I want to ease their pain. I just want them to feel better and end their suffering. That's what a nurse is supposed to do, right? I'm not praying for them to die or anything like that, and I'm certainly not doing anything to interfere with their life support, but when I'm standing there trying to comfort them, that's when a really strange warmth surrounds both of us. I close my eyes for maybe thirty seconds and the warmth passes through me. I can sense their spirit, their personality, detach from their body. Joy fills the room, and I'm happy." She looked up at Emmie. "Can you believe that? I'm *happy* they left their body. That's when the hospital alarms go off and everyone comes running in. When I'm checking their vital signs, I know the patient has passed on—but I'm not sad at all because I know they aren't suffering anymore. Is that... horrible?"

"No, I don't think so," Emmie said softly.

"It's happened to five patients now." Sarah clasped her hands in her lap and rubbed a thumb over the back of her other hand. "I'm sure my coworkers are getting suspicious, maybe wondering, *'What the hell is she doing to those patients?'* but I swear I'm not doing anything harmful. I don't pull the plug or pray they'll die. I'm just meditating and trying to surround them with light to comfort them. That's all."

"I believe you." Emmie adjusted her position on the couch, inching a little closer to her. "Let me ask you a question. Do you see any of the spirits as they pass on?"

"No. Nothing like that. Just the sensations. I feel their spirit moving out as if I've somehow released them from their bodies."

"Do any of them try to communicate with you? Talk to you or try to touch you?"

"No. There's just the feeling that they're not hanging around in this world anymore. Is that anything like what you experience with your gift?"

"It's not a gift," Emmie said in a hard voice. "Trust me. The things I see are like your worst nightmare."

Sarah's posture slumped and her lips pressed tight into a grimace.

You're freaking her out, Em. Go easy. Emmie's face relaxed. "I would love to have a pleasant spirit experience for a change."

"So yours are really scary?"

"Very."

"You see evil things? Demons?"

"No. Dead kids."

Sarah's expression didn't change, but she clasped her hands more tightly.

She's thinking about taking off. I don't blame her.

Emmie continued anyway, "Only dead kids, and then only the ones who have died violently or by suicide. Believe it or not, a lot of kids commit suicide. I don't see anybody else. No adults, no smiling angels of light. Just the most horrible things you could ever imagine. So you see, it's definitely not a gift."

"That's awful," Sarah said, under her breath. Were her eyes shining with tears of sympathy? "Do you see them... all the time?"

Emmie shook her head. "No. Not so much anymore. But I lie to people, and say that I never do, and that's not true either."

"Do you think they want to tell you something?"

"I don't know what they want. I just wish I wouldn't see them anymore."

Emmie couldn't help glancing back at the door to Mary's old apartment. Sarah twisted in her seat and her eyes widened.

Emmie laughed. "There's nothing here." *Another lie.* "But what can I do for you, really?"

"I guess I'm just wondering if my feelings are... real. I'm so confused. Do you have any advice?"

"Yeah." Painful memories flooded Emmie's mind. "Keep your mouth shut. Don't tell anyone about it. Nobody's going to understand it, no matter how well you explain it. And those who do listen to you are probably just humoring you."

"But *you* don't think I'm crazy, do you? Or making this up?"

Emmie studied her. "Well, you *do* have purple hair. That's pretty much a giveaway." She laughed. "No, of course not. Do you think *I'm* crazy?"

"No." Sarah took a deep breath. "That's why I thought you're the only person who might understand me."

"I don't feel the same thing as you. Your experiences sound... kinder. I don't know what advice to give, except to accept it as a good thing?"

Something thumped against the floor behind Emmie. She glanced back at the torn wallpaper.

"Uh-oh." Sarah's eyes widened. "You see something back there? If you're seeing a dead kid, don't spook me."

Emmie laughed. "No. I told you, there's nothing like that." *I need to sell the house, girl!*

"Well, I don't want to take up too much of your time." Sarah picked up her bag. "I'm sure you've got a lot to do with moving in and everything."

"I can take that." Emmie held out her hand for the glass, which Sarah handed over.

Sarah nodded at the wall. "Remodeling?"

"I don't know if you'd call it that. I was just ripping down some wallpaper back there. A couple of friends did the rest and then painted. Still lots to do."

"Oh, you know, I've got a better way of doing that if you're just tearing it off by hand. I've done some remodeling with my parents over the years. If you want, I can help you with that?"

Emmie shrugged. "I could definitely use the help, but I don't want you to take advantage of you."

"Not at all." Sarah shrugged disarmingly. "Maybe this is a good chance to make up for some of that lost time in high school when everything was so messed up."

Emmie smiled. "I would appreciate that. I thought everyone in town would cross the street to avoid me."

They started moving toward the door.

"And we don't need to talk about spirits anymore if it makes you feel uncomfortable," Sarah said. "I just wanted to share this with someone."

"Stop by Saturday morning, if you're not working," Emmie said. "Some friends will be over helping me."

"Sure. I'm off work, and I'll bring along some tools we'll need."

They exchanged phone numbers and Sarah looked back at her white minivan in the driveway. "I better get back home. I work the evening shift tonight."

"Bye, Sarah."

Emmie watched Sarah drive away, then sat outside on the front steps, listening to the leaves rustle in the surrounding trees. Branches creaked and swayed. No birds chirped.

❦ 9 ❧

The card table in the living room had become Emmie's makeshift workspace. She stared at her laptop screen, which showed the photo of a flowery meadow. No point in trying to work. Everything she could do required an internet connection.

Her ears buzzed. The eerie silence of the house replaced the constant rumble of the Los Angeles traffic. She didn't remember it being that quiet before, although everyone was gone now.

She left the card table and went into the kitchen to make her favorite drink—a Brazilian mix called a *caipirinha*, made from cachaça, sugar and limes. It had become her favorite drink after dating a Brazilian man for a few weeks; after their brief fling ended, that one drink had survived. Most restaurants didn't have a *caipirinha* on the menu, so the popular substitute was a margarita. Similar, yet not quite the same.

The ingredients sat on her counter. She'd found the cachaça bottle earlier packed away, lovingly wrapped within a cashmere sweater—one of the few prized possessions she'd brought back with her from LA.

She whipped the ingredients together in the blender and

poured the resulting mix into a glass. Plenty for two people, but no one to share it with.

"*Saúde*." Emmie took a sip. Paulo, her Brazilian flame, had told her that in his country's voodoo, macumba, they routinely left cachaça bottles and cigars under trees at crossroads to appease the *orixás*, or African gods.

Maybe that would work with the Hanging Girl.

The cool, sweet taste threw her mind back to the club scene in Los Angeles and all the outings with her coworkers. So far from that now. It had been a wonderful time away from Minnesota, but she didn't particularly miss anyone.

The emptiness of the kitchen was a stark contrast to how her mom had kept things. She had had the counters full of gadgets and sets of knives.

Better to stop thinking about all that, Em.

She was a survivor, after all. *Right, Emmie?* She could bounce back from anything. She had survived that soulless job in LA and a life she now realized had been lonely, and now she would start over. Nothing to show for all that hard work either. No really close friends, no family, no possessions. The expenses of living in the big city and her social life had taken their toll. She had moved back into her parents' house like every other down-on-their-luck twenty-something.

You've got friends. Emmie took another sip. Sarah's visit had strangely helped, especially as she had thought she would meet with nothing but hostility. A new friend? Then there were John and Mary and, sort of, Robert. She wasn't *completely* alone.

She walked around the living room, sipping her caipirinha and stopping at each of the four pictures John and Mary had hung up on the walls. One picture showed her and Mary a long time ago, sitting on the steps of the house with arms around each other as if they would be best friends for the rest of their lives despite their age difference. Maybe it wouldn't be so far from the truth.

The youthful exuberance of life in the eyes of the child she'd been...

She moved onto the next picture. A decorative display with the words "HOME SWEET HOME" carved in capital letters, each letter made from colorful bows and ribbons. A cute piece, like something her mother might have put up on the wall.

Another picture showed a group of people, most of whose names she'd forgotten. Kids who had banded together one summer to form a baseball team. She'd had just enough friends at that time to make it work. A wonderful summer.

She stopped at the last picture—a family portrait of Emmie and her parents. She remembered taking the picture at Mary and Robert's wedding shortly after Frankie had died. It had been so strange back then to see Mary without Frankie nearby.

So much energy, that boy...

Plenty of things in Green Hills to haunt her for the rest of her life.

Emmie listened to the silence again. None of the footsteps echoing through the hallways or the voices of her parents or the blaring TV. Nothing much left in the house to remind her of the people she'd loved and the time they'd spent together there. Nothing except the empty shell of the house itself.

"This is exactly what I was afraid of. You're talking to yourself now, Em. Be careful."

Her heart ached as she took another sip of her drink and wished she could truly start over. Blocking everything from her mind would be so freaking wonderful.

Something thumped in the distance. Her body tensed and she stared in the direction of the sound. The kitchen floor.

It's an old house. The rotting thing is probably just slowly falling apart.

Emmie gulped down half of her drink.

Hell with that, you know it's her. Bug Eyes.

Another thump as the refrigerator rumbled to life.

No, see? Just your nerves. The girl can't still be in the house. She'll have moved on by now, right? How long can a spirit hang around, anyway? No pun intended.

Emmie walked back to the kitchen and stood in front of the refrigerator. She listened for any other strange noises. Nothing.

Draining the glass of *caipirinha*, she stared out the kitchen window into the front yard. The sun had gone down, and she had switched on the porch light earlier, as if someone might pay her a visit at that time of night.

As she stared across the open lawn, the porch light went out and the yard went black. Nothing was visible outside except a streetlight half a block away.

"Some things never change." The porch light's fuse must have blown. Nothing new. It had been that way for years. Strange that her parents had never fixed the electrical problems.

She knew the breaker box well, having reset it many times over the years. It was down in the basement, in the back corner of the laundry room. The breaker had tripped at odd times without explanation. Sometimes even turning on a desk lamp would trip it, even if it had worked fine for ages. Unpredictable.

John had said that during an inspection of the place the electrician had called attention to the fact that the house was a hundred years old, and that the wiring was dangerously in need of repair. The current fuse box desperately required an upgrade, but she didn't have money for that.

The refrigerator rumbled in the background, just as something thumped against the floor directly beneath her feet.

Her ears perked up, and she stopped breathing as a frigid chill passed through her. The basement.

Nothing's down there, Em.

She hadn't gone down into the basement since she'd arrived, and she hadn't intended to go down there until the next day; but if the front porch light had gone out, then the upstairs bedrooms would be out too. For some reason, the electricians long ago had connected them.

So if she wanted to sleep in her own bed that night, there was no getting around it. She had to go down and reset the breaker.

Setting her glass down on the counter, she walked across the kitchen to the open door into the basement. Another thump, as if someone were slamming a fist into the floor. Had the girl ever made noises like that? Sometimes. Yet another thump, although not as loud, and then another. Several more hard thumps, moving across the floor of the kitchen as if someone were stepping across the basement's ceiling.

Emmie forced in a breath. She glanced back at the *caipirinha* mix and considered chugging down another glassful before venturing downstairs. No, she could do this without more alcohol. What was she afraid of, anyway? She had seen so many things over the years that would have sent most people into an institution. This would be easy. The girl must have moved on by now.

"Oh, hell with it." Emmie turned and stared into the basement. She flipped the light on. From somewhere, a whisper floated up like someone gasping for air.

She took a step down. The sounds stopped.

"I'm coming," Emmie said, "so you better not mess with me." Silence. Nothing. Nobody.

Of course. What did she expect she would see?

Her, but she must have gone away. The only thing left in that house were the terrifying childhood memories.

Had a homeless person broken in and moved into the basement? Happened all the time in Los Angeles. The house *had* sat empty for years. Someone could have made it their home, but John would have checked before Emmie moved in.

But maybe John hadn't checked the basement. Why wouldn't he have gone down there? It was only dark and scary as hell. A good place to hide if a homeless person didn't mind the damp air and noisy ghosts.

"If someone's down there," Emmie said, "get the hell out of

my house right now or I'll call the police. You've only got one chance."

Her words hung in the air as silence flooded in again. Hopeful words, because she would rather have dealt with a squatter than—

The Hanging Girl popped into her mind. That horrible grin, the corners of her mouth stretching wide, and the tongue lolling out as if she were making a funny face. Her wide eyes that never blinked. Bulging white eyes that held an eternal scream. Bug Eyes.

"If that's you, Bug Eyes, I'm a lot older now and I've seen a lot more shit. You're going to have to do better than some dumb-ass thumps to scare me out of here. I'm coming down, and you better stay out of my way."

Emmie took a few more steps down and slowed.

Not as easy as I thought. Emmie shuddered. *Geez, Em, are you going to jump every time the floor creaks in this house? I've already told you, it's probably just the woods settling or the pipes rattling.*

Another thump came from the bottom of the stairs, then a squeak like a tennis shoe grinding against a newly shined floor. A new whisper floated through the air.

Another squeak. Maybe she had rats. *Or a homeless person with pet rats using the bathroom, causing the pipes to rattle, and they tripped the breaker to scare me off. Sure, it makes sense.* The bug-eyed Hanging Girl out in the backyard had nothing to do with it.

Emmie took more steps toward the bottom, moving more slowly as she continued. Her feet squeaked on every step.

The light switch to the laundry room and basement was ahead, against the far wall at the edge of the light coming down from the stairway. She would have to reach out into the darkness a few feet in order to flip it.

"I'm not scared."

Oh shit, yes, she was. Her heart pounded as she extended her hand.

Her skin bristled in the darkness, and she remembered the

childish rhyme from her kindergarten class that had always soothed her during an encounter.

"Now I lay me down to sleep, I pray the Lord my soul to keep."

What the hell do those words mean, anyway?

Before she touched the switch, something caught her gaze in the darkness to her left. A few feet away stood the faint outline of a person.

❧ 10 ❧

Emmie gasped. She flipped on the lights and the person transformed into a broken lamp with a shade perched on the stairs leading up to Mary's old apartment.

She let out a short laugh as her racing heart slowed. "See, Em, no ghosts."

The webbing of a cracked gray stone wall faced her straight ahead. Behind it, the spare bathroom Mary and Frankie had used.

Another thump to Emmie's right, just around the corner. Her pulse throbbed again.

She turned into the laundry room with wide eyes and scanned the area. No homeless person. No rats. No spirits. She stepped in further and followed the thick, black metal pipes along the wall and across the ceiling. They ran under the kitchen floorboards, and as she stared, one pipe lurched to life and rattled.

With a burst of energy originating in some unknown source, the pipe shook and slammed against the ceiling.

Emmie laughed. "Just a crappy old house."

Passing the washer and dryer, she walked to the far wall

where the breaker box hung. At least she wouldn't have to go to the laundromat to wash her clothes.

She opened the box and found the tripped breaker. She had gone through that same process many times as a teenager, and each time it had sent her heart beating wildly as the noises and shadows stirred her imagination. Not always, but sometimes, it had been more than just shadows. Sometimes it had turned out to be the girl standing in the corner watching Emmie. But then her parents had been home— watching TV upstairs or doing household work. Now she was alone. She took a deep breath and reset the breaker for the lights.

Keeping her eyes on the floor, she turned back toward the stairs. Safer that way. She spotted a shadow rushing past her near the stairway entrance.

"That better not be you, Bug Eyes." Emmie reached out to the light switch at the bottom of the stairs and hesitated before shutting it off. She pulled her hand away. "No, I'm leaving it on tonight."

As she hurried up the stairs, she stomped her feet to make as much noise as she could. Drown out all that other crap that might be going on behind her. Her skin crawled all the way to the top.

"Now I lay me down to sleep, I pray the Lord my soul to keep..."

Emmie reached the top of the stairs and turned left through the open door into the kitchen. Another loud thump against the kitchen floor beneath her feet. Almost as if a body had slammed into the ceiling of the basement.

"Pipes," Emmie said, "just pipes this time." She slammed the basement door shut and caught her breath before gazing toward the blender. "How about another drink, Em? Don't mind if I do."

She poured the leftover *caipirinha* mix into a glass. When it touched her lips, she glanced back at the door. A shadow passed over the light coming in through the bottom.

Her body shuddered, and she fumbled with the glass in her hands.

"No!"

It slipped from her fingers and shattered on the floor. Glass shards fanned out over the linoleum. Her drink splashed over her shoes and ankles. She froze in place and surveyed the damage. Tears welled up in her eyes as she took a careful step toward the living room. Glass crunched beneath her feet. At least she hadn't taken off her shoes yet.

Another mess to take care of tomorrow.

Too tired to pick it up now.

Across the living room, she stopped at the doorway to take off her shoes. Might as well go to sleep now.

An object stuck out of a box beside the door. An antique wooden musical jewelry box she'd spotted on her dad's work-bench in the basement one afternoon as a child. After she asked about it, her dad handed it to her, admitting that he'd found it in the corner of the attic. A discarded item from the previous owner? A nostalgic piece she'd held onto all her life for no particular reason other than it reminded her of playing with Frankie and her childhood.

She dug it out and studied the inlaid design of birds and a musical motif on the lid. Everything she knew about the music box she'd learned from the internet and a few minutes of research. A Reuge Swiss musical jewelry box made sometime in the early 1900s. She opened the lid, but no music played—she'd let the spring wind down from the last time she'd played it. Two velvet-lined compartments divided the top section, and a small metal handle sat inside the right side. She wound it and played the only song it would ever play: a tinny old Italian tune called "O Sole Mio".

Sliding the two upper halves apart revealed a "secret" compartment below the other two. Just a larger, red, velvet-lined area she'd used over the years to store her necklaces and earrings.

Someone had etched the word "AH" in the wood along one side. The initials of the previous owner?

She let the simple music play as she started up the stairs. It still worked. Must have been as old as the house. She hadn't appreciated it while growing up, but now it amused her. The music echoed through the hallway, and she made her way to her room to prepare for bed.

She enjoyed the melody. It soothed her. Or maybe that was just the alcohol doing its job.

As she placed the music box on the small bedside table, something on the floor caught her eye. A tarot card lying face up near the wall. The Tower.

She picked it up and dusted it off. Maybe the last piece of Frankie's life left in the house. How many years had it been since they'd played with those cards?

Too tired to do the math.

She laid the card next to the music box and climbed into bed. *Too tired to turn off the light either.* She pulled the sheets up over the side of her face to block the light.

With the music still playing, her mind wandered back to what she had seen in the basement. No *real* sign of the Hanging Girl. She could explain away everything so far. Just the pipes knocking and shadows, and a house that should have been torn down a long time ago.

Maybe the Hanging Girl was truly gone.

Mixing with the "O Sole Mio" melody she'd listened to so many times from the music box, the house's wood frame squeaked, and the wind whistled through the cracks around the window. She would be all right, as long as she didn't panic.

Keep calm, Em. Just count sheep and let the alcohol do its trick.

Another surge of wind pushed against the window and through the cracks around her window frame. The air rushed in, and her eyes locked on to the music box. The Tower card fluttered on her nightstand, then flipped up to face her, coming to a rest against the side of the music box.

What are the odds, Em?
No math tonight.

She closed her eyes and faded into sleep. "O Sole Mio" and a burning tower blurred into her dreams.

❦ 11 ❦

The morning sun filtered in between the rows of blinds over her window. The house was quiet and still. She had dreamed about walking along an ocean beach with her friends. So nice. A handsome guy had even walked by her side and laughed at her jokes.

Had to be a dream if the guy was handsome *and* laughed at her jokes.

She held on to the dream as long as she could as she sat up in bed. The digital clock on the nightstand read 8:15.

Climbing to her feet, she trudged into the bathroom to shower and dress. She moved in a daze as she finished and saun-tered downstairs to have breakfast. As she crossed the living room, she spotted a shard of glass on the floor.

Oh shit, I forgot. She put on her shoes and approached the kitchen. Glass had scattered in every direction, even halfway across the living room, and some tiny pieces were barely visible against the wood floor.

No broom. "Dammit."

She groaned and kicked the larger pieces into one pile. Great way to start the morning. She wet some paper towels from the kitchen and used her shoe to gather the smaller shards. Good enough for now. Her eyes strained to locate any stray pieces.

I'll find them all right—during a barefoot midnight run to the refrigerator.

Her cellphone dinged across the room.

Scanning the floor for more shards of glass, she stepped over to her card table desk and read her messages. A few had come in while she slept. Two friends from California wishing her the best of luck in her new home.

Yeah, everything's going wonderful. She sighed.

The newest message was from Mary, wanting to know if Emmie could stop by the cafe and have breakfast with her.

Emmie glanced over at the piles of glass on the kitchen floor.

She texted back, *Be there soon.*

Without hesitation, she grabbed her keys and hurried outside, slamming the door behind her like a teenager after fighting with her parents. She squealed the tires as she took off from the driveway and barreled over some potholes in the street. John's wise words of law enforcement filled her mind: *Slow the hell down.* She paid no attention.

She had calmed herself by the time she parked in front of Mary's cafe. With the engine off, she sat and watched the cars pass by along the main road through town. How many of them were people she'd grown up with?

A man in a dark suit and a woman in a gray skirt walked by without a glance. She waited until they were out of sight before she got out of the car and entered Mary's cafe.

The delicious odor of coffee and pastries took her mind off the house issues. Mary and Robert were helping customers in a short line at the cash register, while a petite girl just out of her teens or in her early twenties replenished sugar bowls and took cups and dishes away. Patrons occupied most of the tables. Two people stood in line ahead of Emmie, but she waited patiently and watched the couple work.

Mary's face lit up when she saw Emmie, but then her expression turned to concern. "Didn't get much sleep last night?"

"Not enough."

"What happened?"

Emmie glanced at the other customers. The woman right before her was watching from the corner of her eyes. It could wait. "Oh, just the stress of moving, I guess."

"It'll be difficult," Mary said, "but it'll be just fine."

Mary helped the other customers, and Robert avoided eye contact even though he only stood a few feet away. Not even a smile or a nod to her. He focused on filling the orders that Mary was taking at the cash register. His apron was already spoiled with coffee stains.

After serving the customers in the line, Mary took a deep breath and shook her head. "Sorry about that! We suddenly got busy. Just taking it easy today?"

"Well, I'm planning to make a stop at the cemetery. I haven't visited my parents' grave site in a long time, or Frankie's."

Mary's smile softened. "Give him my love, won't you?"

"I will."

The cafe's door opened again, and another small group of customers walked in.

Mary frowned. "Oh dear, I may not have much time to talk this morning. What would you like? Anything at all. It's on me."

"Thank you, Mary. A croissant? And I could really use a French Vanilla—"

"—iced coffee." Mary chuckled. "Coming right up." She stopped the petite girl by the arm. "This is Natalie, by the way, our trusty assistant. Natalie, this is Emmie—and she gets unlimited coffee for free here, all right?"

Natalie smiled and nodded, looking closely at Emmie for a moment as if committing her face to memory so as never to charge her and then moving on.

Robert, on the other hand, still hadn't seen Emmie or had pretended not to.

"Thanks, Mary." Emmie stepped away as more customers moved in.

Emmie glanced around the walls of the cafe. One sign said, "FREE WI-FI: Password: Sunshine." That might come in handy if she didn't get internet soon. Dozens of pictures and rustic wall artwork across the walls gave the place a country feel.

She leaned in and focused on one photo nearby. Mary and Robert stood out in front of their cafe with their arms around each other. In the background stood a dark shadowy figure, a very faint silhouette off to the side. A child. The way the child was posed startled her. Something about the angles, and the arms, and the way it bent its neck. Frankie? He raised his arm as if to wave at the camera. Something he would've done.

Impossible, but that's him. The camera had captured his spirit—unless only she could see him. She didn't dare tell Mary about it.

"Here you go."

Emmie jumped as Mary came up beside her with the order. "Oh, thank you so much, Mary. I really appreciate it."

"Quite all right. I put an extra pastry in the bag for later. I was hoping we could talk this morning, but I'm afraid I'm too busy now. It's wonderful to see you. Have a pleasant time getting yourself reacquainted with the town."

"I will. Thank you again."

Emmie walked out to her car.

Time to relax in the cemetery.

❧ 12 ❧

Finn placed the digital audio recorder down by the edge of the gravestone, far enough below the grass so it would be out of sight. He scanned the cemetery for anyone who might be watching him. The groundskeeper was still mowing near the front, but he was within view. He had repeatedly glanced over while Finn set up his equipment earlier that morning. Another curious onlooker. Always one.

He didn't blame them. He always attracted attention when recording. Most of the time, those who questioned him laughed after he gave the explanation and then left him alone, but occasionally someone was offended by his presence or worse. One elderly woman had accused him of devil worship. She'd screamed Bible verses at him until he'd given up and left. Even followed him in her car until he'd left the town.

Devil worship. Finn rolled his eyes.

He'd taken the equipment and devices from his trunk and placed them strategically around the gravesite. It was enough to stir anyone's curiosity.

One grave held his interest that morning. Franklin Gallagher. A long-shot chance for a ghost sighting, but the story interested him. The house where he'd lived interested him more. The Hanging House.

He glanced at his own clothes. Usually when he went out to record, he dressed more professionally. A well-dressed man with a friendly smile generally received less sideways glances than a man in jogging bottoms and a graphic t-shirt with a corporate logo scrawled across the front, but his good clothes were in the washer. No time to be picky.

The groundskeeper paused on his riding lawnmower and glanced over in Finn's direction again.

Now you're going to come over and ask me what the hell am I up to, aren't you?

If Finn were investigating a house, then of course, he would ask permission from the owners before setting anything up, but this was a public cemetery, after all. He wasn't really *bothering* anybody. No one to disturb.

Stepping back, he slipped on the headphones, testing the audio input by tapping his toe against the side of the recorder. *Thud, thud.* Everything was working properly.

He set up the thermal imaging camera next, testing it by aiming it across the area above the gravesite. He locked it onto the tripod and watched the monitor for any signs of aberrations. Nothing yet, but the air was warm, and that was to be expected. It would be better to come back at night when the air was cool. The heat signatures would display better, but that wasn't possible without trespassing.

After making some adjustments and starting to record the data, he sat down on top of a wide rectangular gravestone behind him. The birds chirped overhead, and the sun peeked through the rustling leaves around him. A pleasant day. Perfect for his hobby. He likened it to birdwatching, except he hadn't yet seen his bird. His target was elusive, and maybe impossible to capture, but he would try. No hurry. He had all day Friday and the entire weekend to hunt for spirits. A stark contrast to the hectic world of photojournalism and a contributing editor job.

Here there was nobody to stand in his way, and no need to worry about deadlines and edits until Monday morning.

While recording a longer stretch of thermal imaging data, he pulled out his Nikon DSLR and snapped several photos in all directions around the area. Better to get as much data as possible to verify and cross-reference anomalies between devices. A thermal aberration might strike him as unusual, but by taking pictures from different angles he could rule out other sources for the anomaly that almost always turned out to be natural causes. At the same time, the biggest surprises came after failing to find a plausible explanation. Those unexplained oddities were the driving force behind his hobby.

He aimed the Nikon back toward the groundskeeper who hadn't gotten much further than the last time. At that moment, a police car turned into the cemetery. He lowered the camera. The car circled around through the narrow winding roads and headed straight toward him. The cops had approached him a few times over the years, but he'd never had any trouble after they understood what he was doing. Still, it was better not to have any electronics in his hand to prevent misunderstandings. He placed his camera on the ground next to his other equipment.

Doubtful that the cop just *happened* to make a pass through the cemetery. The groundskeeper must have called him.

Finn glared at the stocky man on the riding lawnmower. *Good job, sir. You've performed an admirable duty to the fine dead citizens of this town. You've protected them from a man with a camera. Oh, what horrible, vile deeds he could have done if they had allowed him to use it.*

The police car pulled up beside him, and the officer stepped out. An older cop with thick-rimmed glasses and a focused stare. Finn kept his hands away from his pockets, and the officer had the same *"What the hell are you doing?"* expression as every other person who'd ever questioned him.

"And what's going on over here?" the officer asked.

"Research, Officer. I'm a paranormal investigator, it's a hobby of mine."

The officer's eyebrows shot up. "A hobby? That's a far cry from collecting postage stamps. Are you from around here?"

"No, sir, Edina. A suburb of Minneapolis."

"I know where Edina's at. You're a long way from home. Can I see some ID?"

"Yes, sir." Finn carefully removed his wallet from his back pocket and handed his license to the officer who studied it and then handed it back.

"What brings you out this way, Mr. Adams?"

Finn considered some smartass responses but held back. *Better play it straight.* "Ghosts. I travel around the state and record paranormal activities."

The officer nodded. Finn read the name on his badge. Officer Ratner.

"What makes you think there are ghosts around here?" Officer Ratner folded his arms over his chest.

"Just from the stories I've read. About the Hanging House, in particular. I'm sure you've heard of it."

Officer Ratner grinned. "Yes, I have. So what are you planning to do at the cemetery today?"

Finn gazed down at his devices in the grass. "I'm hoping to record several things. Video, audio, thermal, magnetic. Paranormal evidence."

"Nothing destructive, I hope."

"No, sir."

"No digging or taking samples, correct?"

"Absolutely not, sir."

"Would you mind removing your glasses?"

Finn took them off and squinted as the officer stepped in closer, staring into his eyes. "Have you been drinking or taking any drugs?"

"Recently?"

Officer Ratner smirked. "Answer the question."

"No, sir. Nothing like that."

"I don't mind people inquiring about the town's past, but I'm not one to put up with any shenanigans. Are we clear?"

Shenanigans? "Yes, sir."

Officer Ratner nodded again. "What do you plan on doing with all this data after you're done?"

"Well, I generally go through it to see if there's any activity. Sometimes I get lucky and run across something out of the ordinary."

"That's a lot of equipment for someone who's just doing it as a hobby. Why search for ghosts?"

"Good question. I think it's an existential issue that everyone has. Is there life after death? Does our consciousness survive after we die, and if so, are we able to record that in a form that can be scientifically analyzed and verified?"

Officer Ratner waved his hand. "Okay, that's enough. I get it. Just make sure you clean up after you're done and don't disturb anything or anyone. We like our ghosts where they are. Understand?"

"Yes, sir."

The cop glanced over the devices on the ground one more time before getting back in his car. Finn stood in place but leaned against one of the gravestones while the officer chatted on his radio for a few minutes. The groundskeeper had paused his mower and watched them from a distance.

Officer Ratner didn't look over or acknowledge him as he drove out of the cemetery. The groundskeeper continued mowing the grass, now without looking over at Finn.

And Finn's heart continued racing even after the officer was gone. He wasn't doing anything wrong, but even being approached by the police for the simplest of reasons racked his nerves.

Finn picked up his thermal camera and checked the monitor. Still no sign of anything. Maybe he should have asked for permission to come at night, but the cop would probably have thrown him out of the place at the request. He looked over the pictures he'd taken. Nothing yet, but he would inspect it closer after he returned home.

Another car entered the cemetery and drove along the same path the cop had taken. It came straight toward him and parked behind his car.

A pretty, dark-haired girl sat in the driver's seat. His eyes met hers for a moment. She seemed to scowl at him, as if he'd done something to upset her too.

"Great," he mumbled and walked back to his equipment to continue with his research.

13

Emmie pulled into the front gate of the cemetery, circled up a short hill and curved around the war memorial towering over her. She headed to the back of the cemetery and stopped near her parents' grave. The wheels on her side crossed over onto the grass a little, but she avoided driving near the graves. *Don't want to upset the tenants below.*

Frankie's grave was less than a hundred feet away. A tall, dark-haired man with a camera was circling his gravestone and taking pictures. His clothes reminded her of someone who might be on their way to a college kegger party: a loose black t-shirt and jogging pants. He turned away when he spotted her watching him, but she kept an eye on him while he retrieved something from the back seat of his silver Ford Fusion.

What the hell was he doing over there?

She sat in the grass in front of her parents' grave site and stared at the polished front surface of the two-foot-wide granite marker. Their names were etched into the stone side by side with a carving of an angel, his wings stretched out, in the middle. The inscription was simple and heartfelt. *In loving memory of Mom and Dad. Shannon Fisher. Edward Fisher.*

Emmie turned her face to the sun and closed her eyes. She listened to the leaves rustle in the trees around her and a lawnmower rumble nearby.

It wasn't supposed to be like this. She'd left home seven years earlier with no intent to return to Green Hills—sick of the insults and stares—but she'd never thought anything like this could happen. So sudden and devastating. Never had she felt so alone in the world. She'd wanted to get away from everything right out of high school. Go to college, have an adventure, forget her past. They weren't supposed to be gone before she'd had a chance to find herself. They were supposed to be there when she crawled back home years later, battered and bruised; an older, wiser, woman. The Prodigal Daughter.

The lawnmower hummed more loudly in the distance. She opened her eyes and located the source. The groundskeeper's lawnmower circled and weaved between gravestones. It was Mr. Gardner, her retired seventh grade English teacher. Ironic that he'd taken the job of cemetery groundskeeper now. It didn't seem fitting for an intelligent man with vast literary knowledge. She'd enjoyed listening to his stories in class. He'd traveled the world and loved to talk about it.

The man near Frankie's grave set up another piece of equipment, this time connecting it to a tripod. Not a camera this time, but a smaller square device. He put on headphones and held out a long microphone into the air.

She looked back down at her parents' gravestone and recounted her life in California for them, as if they didn't already know all the details up in heaven. Still, she rushed through a five-minute condensed version, even defending her bad choices and the failed relationships that had put her on a roller-coaster ride ending in heartbreak.

"Just part of life's shitty journey." Emmie's eyes watered. "Got to do my time just like everyone else, right? But haven't I completed my sentence by now?"

She spilled her feelings about moving back into the house, and the hope of finally moving on with her life. But that wasn't going to happen so soon, was it?

When the man at Frankie's grave started packing up his equipment, Emmie watched him more closely. He had an air of confidence about him, like he was going about some highly scientific experiment that nobody else would understand. He turned his back to her most of the time, as if he knew she was watching, and carefully placed each piece into the trunk of his car.

After the man got into his driver's seat, and it appeared he would leave soon, Emmie said goodbye to her parents with wet eyes and walked the short distance over to Frankie's grave. The man glanced at her after she sat down in front of his gravestone, but he didn't stare. *Good. Just be on your way.*

Mary had purchased a lavish sculpture of an angel standing on a cloud for Frankie's memorial. Franklin Donald Gallagher. The dates revealed he'd died at seven years old. More exactly, seven years and forty-seven days. She had calculated it.

"It's been a long time, Frankie." Emmie reached out and touched his name. "Sorry for not stopping by lately, but I had to get away from this horrible town. I'm glad I helped find you back then, but I wish I could have done more before, so none of this shit would have happened." Emmie chuckled once. "I wish I could talk to you in person. I'm sure we'd be friends even now. I moved back into the house, and of course I'm hearing Bug Eyes. It sounds like her. You'd think that after all these years she'd give me a break, but no.

"I hope you're enjoying your time up in heaven...

"Times are tough now, Frankie. I don't know how long I'll be able to stand living in this town, but I'll give it my best shot. I hope Bug Eyes won't show up because I only have to stay here long enough to sell the house and get that money before I can take off. That'll be a real trick, I guess. Who the hell wants to buy a haunted house? I wish Mom and Dad had never bought it. Maybe none of this crap would have happened if they hadn't. Maybe, I don't know. Do you think they knew about the ghost stories before they bought it?" Emmie chuckled again, inside— without smiling. "Yeah, me too. That's probably *the main reason* they bought it. Just couldn't pass up an opportunity like that. Crazy shit. Now I just need to find someone nuttier than them to take it off my hands."

Emmie stroked the grass with her fingers and stopped on a solid object. A spherical man-made shape. She dug it out from the dirt and held it to the light. A marble? She cleared away the dirt from one side with her thumb and the light struck a smooth, glassy surface.

Looks just like Frankie's old marbles. The swirl of blues, reds, and yellows were unmistakable. Murano marbles from his collection. She ran her fingers through the dirt again and snagged two more. Who had dropped them there?

She brushed the dirt off each one before slipping them into her pocket.

A crow screeched in a nearby tree.

"Well, I guess I'll head back home in a bit. At least I have a place to go. What would you do in a situation like that? Would you get back up and climb the mountain again, or just stay put and call it a day? Yeah, me too. Nothing's going to keep me down. Especially not that crappy house."

A tear flowed down Emmie's cheek. "I love you, Frankie, and I love Mom and Dad. Damn, I wish I could stop seeing ghosts. What a weird thing to have to deal with."

Emmie's fingers ran into another solid object in the grass. Larger and plastic. An electronic device pushed just beneath the surface. She dug it out from the dirt and examined it. A small red light was on. A Digital Audio Recorder like one she used to record college lectures.

She glanced back at the man in the car. The engine was

running, and he was staring into a tablet resting on the steering wheel.

"That's interesting." She stood up with the device and walked over to confront him.

❧ 14 ❧

E mmie knocked on the driver's side window. The man was viewing a photo of the cemetery, zooming into an area in the background, then changing the colors and contrast. Next to him, on the passenger seat, a piece of electronic equipment displayed strings of numbers beside a graph chart.

The man rolled down the window and smiled, though with a suspicious look.

"Hi, sorry to bother you." Emmie held up the digital recorder. "Is this yours?"

The man's eyes widened. "Yes. I left it there on purpose. I'm recording."

"Recording what?"

The man grinned as he accepted the device from her. "It's hard to explain. I'm investigating a death that happened here years ago. I was intending to leave that by the gravesite for a few hours and pick it up later."

"Whose death is that?" Emmie asked, but she already knew the answer.

"A young boy by the name of Franklin Gallagher. I assume you've heard of him, since you were sitting by his grave."

Emmie paused. "Everybody's heard of him."

The man got a curious look on his face. "Do you know anything about him?"

Lie, Emmie. "A little."

The man perked up. "Would you mind talking with me about it?"

"What's your interest in him?"

"I research paranormal activity as a hobby."

"What kind of hobby is that?"

"A very unusual one." The man smiled again. He had some charm.

Emmie nodded. "I see."

"If you can tell me anything about him, I'd greatly appreciate it. I'm also interested in a house in town known as the Hanging House. Have you heard of that place?"

"I've heard of it," she drawled.

"Well, I'd love to hear anything you have to say about it. The boy who used to live there, Franklin, and another possible ghost too."

"Ghosts...?"

"You don't believe in ghosts?"

Emmie held back a laugh. "I'm not sure."

"Well, I think there is actually a lot more to them than just superstitions. There's been a lot of unexplained phenomena that deserve to be verified." He motioned toward the machine. "And I want to be the guy who finally records real scientific evidence of it."

"You want to hunt down a ghost?"

"Not *hunt down*. In this case, I'm more like a wildlife photographer than a hunter. I don't think anybody can really capture a ghost."

She gazed at him for a moment. "Don't be so sure."

The man stared into her eyes, almost as if he had understood something. "Have *you* ever seen a ghost?"

She shook her head. *Keep it casual, Em.* "Can't say I have."

He nodded a few times, still considering her. "Why don't I

give you my card, and if you want to talk about Franklin or local ghost tales, I'd love to hear from you."

Emmie accepted his card. "I'll let you know if I hear of anyone who has seen *ghosts*."

"Thank you." Before she moved away, he added, "Let me ask you something." The man dug through some papers on the passenger seat of his car and pulled up a photo print out of Emmie's house. He held it up to her. "Do you know if this is the Hanging House or not?"

Taking it, Emmie pretended to study it. "I don't think so. No, definitely not it."

The man stared at the picture after Emmie returned it to him. "Really?" He pursed his lips. "Did I get the wrong house?" A slight smile crept across his face. "You know which is the right house, then?"

"I'm not really sure."

A moment of silence hung between them. "Well, thanks for your help. Hope I didn't interfere with your visit to Franklin's grave. I try to stay out of the way."

"You're fine."

The man glanced at the digital recorder. "I should put this back. I'd still like to get audio to analyze later."

Emmie held out her hand. "Sorry, I'll do it. I just thought you forgot it."

The man switched it on, then placed it in her hand. "Thanks. Just a little into the ground so it's out of sight, if you don't mind. I've lost a few of them over the years."

"I'll put it back where I found it." She held up the device.

"Perfect. Thank you."

Emmie scanned all the different electronic devices he had scattered on the passenger seat and in the backseat. "All that stuff is to find ghosts, huh?"

"That's the idea. One of these days I'll find one. I just need to keep searching."

"Well, good luck with your ghosts."

"What's your name, by the way?"

Emmie paused. "Rose." Her middle name would do just fine.

"Thank you, Rose. My name's Finn." He held out his hand to her, and she shook it.

"Nice to meet you," she said.

"Remember to contact me if you find any information about that house. It's a passion of mine."

"I will."

"Have a great day."

"You too." Emmie stepped away from Finn's car, and he took off up the road. After he was out of sight, she stared down at the red light on the face of the audio recorder in her hand.

Awfully trusting guy to leave that with me.

In any case, he was wasting his time if he expected any paranormal activity. No ghosts nearby, at least no child ghosts.

She placed the digital recorder back where she found it, pushing it a little into the grass, just out of sight. She felt sneaky and awkward hiding it, like she was playing an FBI agent trying to trap a criminal. Maybe that was part of the appeal.

Trust me, Finn, you don't want to see any ghosts.

15

The Green Hills Library had always been a place where Emmie could go to escape from the world. She'd made frequent trips there as a child, so as she walked in, the smell of books and the gentle hum of the air conditioner blanketed her like old friends.

Meeting the ghostbuster had done one thing: awakened her need to know more about her own house. She'd avoided listening to all the stories and rumors about how the Hanging Girl had died over the years. Focusing on her had always drawn her closer.

Meditate and communicate, Emmie's mom whispered in her mind.

But she wasn't that scared little girl anymore. It was time to face her fears and find out the truth about how the Hanging Girl had died. Maybe that information didn't even exist anymore.

The girl at the desk looked familiar. Her red hair and glasses stirred Emmie's memory. Someone from her high school class? She stared for a moment, then remembered. She was one of the nice ones. "Jennifer?"

Jennifer looked up from her desk, and her face brightened. "Emmie, hi! I heard you were back in town." Jennifer walked around the desk and gave her a hug. "Are you visiting or moving back for good?"

"I'm not sure yet. I'm fixing up the house now, but I want to sell it."

"It's been sitting empty for a long time. Good luck."

"I'm not surprised to find you working here. You were always reading stuff in your spare time. A real bookworm."

"Yeah, I love books, all right. I'm in heaven here. Are you looking for something good to read?"

"Not exactly. I'm trying to find more information about my house. I mean, from a long way back when it was built. Do we have any information about the town back then, or events from maybe a hundred years ago?"

Jennifer swallowed. "You mean, all the stories? The ghosts?"

"Yes." Emmie rushed to add, "Not that any of it's true."

"No. Of course not." Jennifer was just as quick to dismiss the idea. Too quick. "A lot of old newspapers were digitized recently, so you're in luck. Before that, you'd have to manually scroll through all the microfiche. Technology, right?"

"Perfect. Where's all that?"

Jennifer half turned toward the back of the library. "In the far corner. Weird that you're asking about it. A guy from out of town came in right before you and asked about the same thing. Do you know him?"

The ghost hunter? "I don't think so."

Jennifer smiled and nodded. "I guess the subject of your house comes up in some circles. I hope he respects your privacy."

"I'm not worried."

"He's back there at the machine right now." Jennifer gestured to the far corner. "You'll have to fight him over the one computer we have able to display that info. Sorry."

Emmie looked at the back toward where Jennifer was pointing. "Thank you. It's nice to see you."

Without waiting for a response, Emmie crossed the library,

passing a few individuals hiding out behind books in the corners of the room. She came up behind Finn and hesitated to say anything. Maybe he'd think she was stalking him. *No sense turning back now.*

Maybe he'd already found information about the house and its history.

Before Emmie could say anything, Finn turned. A jolt of panic spread through her. Within the light of the library, Finn's face looked older and wiser. Was it from being surrounded by books?

He mocked a smile. "Oh, it's you. Rose, right?"

The game was up. She sighed. "Not really."

"No..." he agreed. "You're Emmie Fisher, right?"

Emmie bit her lip, embarrassed that he'd caught her deceiving him. "Yes."

He nodded. "Emmie Rose Fisher. I was ninety-five percent sure back at the cemetery, but I left open the possibility that *maybe* someone in town looked like you."

"Sorry."

"No problem. I understand. You need to keep your identity quiet after all the publicity. It must have been difficult growing up with everyone staring at you and whispering behind your back."

"Exactly."

"People think you sense things." He turned fully to face her. "Tell me, am I getting close to any genuine phenomena?"

A man who liked to cut to the chase. "You're closer than you think," she allowed.

His eyes lit up. "Are you referring to the Hanging House?"

"Why don't you tell me first how you got to be interested in this stuff?"

He smirked and narrowed his eyes. "I'll show you mine, if you'll show me yours?"

Sitting on the corner of the desk behind her, she scoffed. "You'll get in trouble for talking like that nowadays."

With a small shrug, he leaned back in the chair, running his hands through his hair and leaving them on his head. "I have an uncle who claimed his dead wife visited him several times after she passed. I thought maybe he'd had too much to drink some nights. But he gave so many details, and I knew my uncle wasn't crazy, so I stayed with him a few nights."

"Did you see anything?"

He shook his head. "No. But...but I *felt* something. It's not proof of anything, but it was enough to make me study cases of haunting. Why not? These stories have persisted since humanity's beginning, I guess. So, if anyone claimed to have seen a ghost, as a journalist I'd go there—asking questions, taking photos. And when you inspect the evidence, it's obvious most people are mistaken. Most of the stories are just misunderstandings, the result of faulty wiring or someone's imagination, but then there's those few cases that don't add up."

"What do you mean by those?"

Finn shrugged. "Stuff like my uncle's story. I guess I knew him, and I knew he wasn't hallucinating and didn't believe in this stuff, and that opened my mind to it. Paradoxical, isn't it? And now I want proof."

Emmie smiled. "Visual proof, with all that equipment you carry around?"

"Yes. Call it *scientific* proof. Something more than just a feeling. It's very exciting when I do capture something, but I've always been able to explain away the sightings as natural phenomena, electrical disturbances, pranks, or something else like that." Nodding at her with his chin, he said, "Your turn."

"I hate to talk about it." She threw a glance around. "No one believes it. Or, when people do, it's even worse."

Lowering his arms, perhaps to look more solemn, he said, "I'm all ears, and I promise I won't judge."

"This curiosity about ghosts, like yours, has been a part of my life since I was a kid. My parents were interested in the occult and they encouraged me to explore that side of reality. They weren't *scientific* like you, though."

"What, more like seances, or a reading or automatic writing —stuff like that?"

"Yes. Just about every weekend they were doing something. They had friends from Chicago with the same interests visit every once in a while, and on those days they'd experiment with psychic stuff. ESP, that type of thing."

"That must have been strange, growing up," he mused.

"My parents weren't evil or anything like that. No devil worship or freaky shit—just always trying to communicate with the dead." Emmie laughed. "To me, that's not freaky. *Seeing* the dead all the time, now that's freaky."

Finn grimaced. "You *see* ghosts?"

"Not all of them. I'm sure there's a lot more of them out there, but I only see dead kids. Lucky me. It started with *that* one girl in particular. The one hanging from the big tree in our backyard."

"Are you saying the stories about the girl in your house are real?"

"Yes, I'm saying that. I've seen her in the backyard many times while growing up, and she doesn't just stay in the backyard. She comes in the house too. She used to visit me in my bedroom or down in the basement. Anywhere it was dark. Sometimes I would see her from the corner of my eye, whether or not my parents were there."

"And your parents didn't see her?"

"No."

"Seems unfair," he mused. "They keep calling ghosts, and when they come, you're the one who sees them."

Emmie nodded. "Who knows if that's what happened—if they provoked it? What I know is I had to learn to ignore the ghosts."

"Why?"

"What do you mean, why?" Emmie's face warmed. "I'd wake

up in the middle of the night and see a teenage girl standing next to my bed with long brown hair and an old-fashioned nightgown like something they'd wear on an Old West TV show. Her neck was broken, and she grinned with her tongue out like this." Emmie imitated the Hanging Girl's expression.

"Did she appear like a wisp of smoke or a solid being?" he was quick to ask.

Emmie sighed. At least he wasn't laughing, and he didn't look scared. *He's got his scientific hat on.* "It depends. I used to see her hanging from the tree most of the time. The first time she was like what they show in the movies, a cloudy human form; I could still see through her. But then she became more and more real because I stared at her."

"You say you see other kids as well. Is it always like that?"

"Yes, the more I think about them, the more I notice them. I know it's weird, but I can usually avoid seeing the dead if I just don't focus on them. It's like not noticing the color red until somebody asks you to look for the color red—then you see it all the time, or at least for a while, and then forget about it again."

She watched the subtle motions of his face. He was analyzing her, trying to figure out whether or not she was telling the truth.

"I know it sounds crazy," she said, somewhat annoyed at his scrutiny—*he* had started it.

Finn raised his eyebrows. "I have to admit, it does sound a bit far-fetched, but I guess that's the kind of thing I'm looking to investigate."

That's how it was. They asked, they even accused, then they doubted. Emmie sneered for a moment, then gazed at the newspaper article up on his screen. An old black-and-white picture of her house was below the headline, "Local Girl Finds Missing Boy."

Glancing back at the computer screen, his cheeks flushed. "I'm sorry, I didn't mean for you to see that. I'm not being nosy just for the sake of it—"

She had not gone on reading and let her eyes drop to her

hands instead. "I never wanted to know any of that. They accused me of being involved in his death because I couldn't explain how I knew where to find Frankie."

"How *did* you know?"

"It was easy. We have a back apartment in our house. Frankie and his mom lived there, and we played a psychic game of hide and seek once in a while. After he went missing, all I had to do was focus on him, and I knew where he was. In my mind, I could see him. I knew he was dead before they found him, and I guess that's why everyone thought I was involved somehow. How would I know that information, and where he was?"

Finn shook his head slightly. "I don't know."

Taking a deep breath, Emmie looked back at the article on the computer. "Can I get in there and read that?"

"Absolutely." Finn stood and pulled the chair back for her, then grabbed another chair for himself. They both leaned toward the screen, reading at the same time.

The article said they'd discovered Frankie's naked body in the water, caught in some weeds. She cringed at the details. The autopsy revealed water in his lungs, listing the cause of death as drowning.

The investigation into his death had been routine, as they'd found no sign of foul play. They'd questioned a man named Bobby Norris because he'd been teaching a group of kids to swim in the lake near the beach where Frankie's body was found. Norris had been a swimming instructor from the school, and he'd always taken kids to the lake during good weather rather than teach them at an indoor pool. But Norris had had an alibi; without an accomplice, he could not have drowned Frankie.

Perhaps they'd reserved the harshest questions for Emmie.

How did you know where to find him? How did you know he was dead?

Did you kill him? Did you go swimming with your little friend and drown him?

"*I loved my friend,*" she had sobbed.

Her only alibi had been her parents; she'd been at home with them. They'd been watching reruns of a silly sitcom on TV. But that only made her parents suspects as well.

Did you see your father drowning Frankie?

Did your mother drown Frankie?

How did you know where he was?

Officer John Ratner's name stood out in the article. Her oasis from all the chaos. When others had brought her to tears with the harsh questioning, John had stepped in and protected her, calming her and making her feel safe again.

At the end of another article, the verdict: death by accident. The coroner couldn't have ruled any other way, it said. Passing neighbors had spotted her and her parents in the house all through that afternoon and evening. The medical examiner had placed Frankie's death inside a window of time, but even stretching that window, none of her family could have been out at the lake.

Which left the question in everyone's mind forever: How had the girl known where to find the body?

"Because she knew he swam there," John had finally snarled at reporters and townspeople alike. "She guessed it, that's why. He was told not to go there alone, but he was stubborn. That's all."

John had taken her side like a fierce, wonderful bear. People had stopped asking, but her ordeal in that town had only begun.

"Those were bad times," Emily muttered.

"I can imagine."

"I didn't even want to go outside because people would stare at me. They still stare at me if they remember my past, after all these years. That's why I don't want to talk about it most of the time. That's why I lied to you about my name."

"I get it..."

Emmie narrowed her eyes. "You're not writing a newspaper article on me or anything like that, right?"

"Nothing like that, I promise." He hesitated. "I don't mean

to be rude or insensitive, but in cases of violent deaths, the theory goes that the spirits hang around—"

"I haven't seen Frankie's ghost," she snapped at him. "No."

Finn pursed his lips as he nodded, fidgeting a little in his chair.

"You don't believe me?" Emmie clenched her fists and furrowed her brow.

Finn's eyes widened as he leaned back. "Well, I'm always skeptical. That's just my nature. I don't mean any offense by it. Again, it always comes back to the proof. I do believe in apparitions, but after analyzing so many, I'm at a loss to find more than a couple that are genuine mysteries."

"I'm not lying."

"I'm not saying you are." Finn attempted a smile and narrowed his eyes. "Would you like to know more about the Hanging Girl? Or do you know already?"

"I actually came here to see if there was anything about her. I avoided finding out before."

He reached for the mouse, minimizing the articles about Frankie until he found what he was looking for.

"This article here talks about the Hanging Girl and the story behind it. She was, in fact, found hanging in the tree behind your house around the time the house was being built. Her death was never solved—no one knew whether it was a murder or a suicide. She was the daughter of a rich family, and her parents died shortly before she did. They built the house in 1921 and after her death, her brother lived there until 1937. Someone else bought the house after he died, and then your family did."

"I didn't know all that." She leaned back, looking at him. "It seems so close in time, in a way. I wonder if my parents knew this and never told me?"

Finn tapped some more keys. "That's all that is here, in the old newspapers. Maybe they'll digitize some more." He stood and gathered his things. "I need to get back to the cemetery to pick up my digital recorder. Don't want it closing on me. You put it next to Franklin's grave, right?"

"Right back where I found it."

"Cool. Thank you for that."

She stayed where she was. "Let me know if you find anything."

"I'd need to get your phone number," he said, looking down at her. His eyes bore through hers, no hesitation in them.

Emmie's face warmed. *Am I blushing?* "I guess, as long as you promise not to tell anyone about our conversation."

Finn put his palm over his heart. "I promise."

When he produced his cellphone, Emmie told him her number, and he typed it into his contacts.

"Got it," Finn said. "You still have my card, right? I live down in the cities, in Edina. Feel free to call me anytime you want to talk about the house or ghosts or anything. I wouldn't mind investigating your house or the Hanging Tree, if you would ever consider that."

Emmie shook his hand. "Let me think about it."

"Thanks for talking to me, Rose-or-should-I-say-Emmie." He smiled warmly. "I know that wasn't easy."

"Nice to meet you, Finn."

He turned and left.

Emmie sat at the computer for a few more minutes, reading the article on the Hanging Girl, and stopped at the name Alice Hyde.

Alice Hyde. She'd never known the girl's real name. Still, it didn't change anything. The Hanging Girl, Alice, Bug Eyes, whatever, had ruined *her* life.

Emmie shut down the computer, clearing its memory for the next user. She'd given the traumas of her life enough thought for one day.

🎕 16 🎕

The thunder and lightning strikes grew louder as the night rolled in. Emmie listened to the rain pounding against the bedroom window and to the walls creak as the wind tested the strength of her house.

"Just let the whole thing collapse." Emmie closed her eyes. At least she wouldn't hear any spirits banging around downstairs.

A crack of lightning broke her eyes open again. No sense in trying to go to sleep yet. It was only nine o'clock, but she hung on the edge of that dark, cloudy descent into sleep.

For the first time in weeks, she hadn't drunk a drop of alcohol. Not that she ever drank a lot, but oh God, she loved a little soothing something once in a while to clear her mind.

There's still time. Plenty early to go back down to the kitchen and pour herself one of those *caipirinhas* she loved so much. No? Lots of other possibilities to mix with rum. She'd learned plenty of info from the internet over the years on how to mix different drinks. But today her ingredients were limited. As long as it only involved rum and limes, she was good. Time to make a trip to the store. She pictured herself as a bartender and chuckled. No. Not going to happen.

Her eyelids fell and then opened again after another lightning strike. She might be up for hours if the storm continued at that intensity.

She stared up at the ceiling and connected some familiar lines and cracks spreading out like a giant web.

Some of them might really be spider webs.

The patterns almost formed a work of art, a human face in the way the cracks intersected and looped through the aging ceiling. Just as if looking at the moon and seeing a face there, she had constructed the imaginary face of a protective guard watching over her while she slept.

But now the lines moved, the lips opening and closing and the eyes widening. The cracks spread apart, forming deep creases in the corners of the mouth. It became a face of insanity, staring down at her with a widening jaw full of teeth that erupted beneath its developing flesh.

Emmie's pulse pounded in her ears. She couldn't move or even look away. The thing's lips quivered, drawing blood from the depths of its throat. It smacked them together, and a long thread of bloody saliva dangled from its mouth. The drop stretched out more, stopping inches from her face.

"Go away." Emmie heaved in a deep breath. "Bug Eyes, is that you?"

The face laughed and the long string of saliva broke. A drop of liquid splashed onto Emmie's tongue as she gasped.

She gagged and lurched up from her bed, spitting the blood on the floor. Wiping her mouth, she looked at the back of her hand. A clear liquid—just wet. Staring up at the ceiling, she now only saw the familiar patterns of cracks she recognized from her youth. A bubble of water appeared in one of the cracks and dripped down onto her pillow.

A hard swallow, and she caught her breath. "It's not fair. I don't have any choice, Bug Eyes. I don't have anywhere else to go. I'll get out of here as soon as I can, so you can start in on terrifying the next poor souls trapped in this hellhole. Just stop this shit and let me get on with my life so I can get out of here. Deal?"

Silence. Another drop landed on her pillow.

Emmie moaned.

She grabbed her bed's frame and dragged it out from under the leak. A small plastic trashcan beside her nightstand worked perfectly to collect the water leaking from her ceiling. Another problem to fix.

A drop of water thudded into the bucket, then several more.

"Dammit, Bug Eyes! I'm sick of your shit!"

Emmie stormed out of her room and downstairs to the front door dressed only in her slippers and pajamas. A flashlight sat on the living room floor.

I don't need it. I know where I'm going.

She marched out to her driveway and stopped for a moment, staring at the garage near the back of the house. The Hanging Tree rose above the top of the garage. No need to go back there ever again. But nausea roiled in her stomach.

Branches swayed as a sudden gust of wind swept through her hair. That tree and the girl attached to it had ruined her childhood. She might have had a chance at a normal life if it hadn't been for the constant terror and her inability to protect herself from the Hanging Girl's confrontations. Of course she had begged her parents to have the thing cut down, but they'd refused. The myth was what sold them on the house, and they had practically worshiped that tree. Their prized trophy. Why cut down something so cherished? Emmie would just have to deal with it.

Deal with it.

"Aw, hell." Emmie walked up the driveway toward the garage. Her legs weakened as she approached it.

She rounded the side, inching forward as the tree's dead limbs came into view. A few more steps before the main trunk appeared.

Oh God, if she's there, I'm going to die.

That's ridiculous.

She stopped. Her body slowed as if she had just walked a mile. The sky grew blacker as the clouds rolled in. Was the sun also going down faster than normal?

Come on, girl, just another thing to get through.

She couldn't move. "Now I lay me down to sleep, I pray the Lord my soul to keep. If I should die..." She forced her legs to move and she stepped forward. The massive oak tree filled her field of vision.

The main branch, jutting off almost perpendicular to the trunk, darkened as the night crept in.

No Hanging Girl.

"Leave me the hell alone!" Emmie screamed into the darkness. "Do you think I want to be here? Hell, no! But this is *my* house now and I've put up with you long enough. Do you hear me?"

Emmie stared into the empty air below the branch where the girl had appeared so many times in her childhood. Her skin bristled. At any moment Bug Eyes could appear. But she didn't. Her heart slowed a little.

Better, Em? Nothing in the house last night and nothing here now. Just a leaky roof and a bad dream. She's gone.

Emmie caught herself trembling and took in a deep breath. "I'm not afraid of you, anyway."

She didn't believe herself. Something pulled at her insides, gnawing at her stomach. Looking at it wasn't enough. She wanted to touch the tree and stand under the branch. Something she hadn't even done as a child. She would move into the Hanging Girl's space and claim it.

She stepped forward as the anxiety welled up inside her. The voice in her head was screaming, *Get the hell out of there. Run!* She continued and stretched out her hand toward it.

A tug of war clutched her muscles. The fight-or-flight response kicked in.

Nothing there, except her fear.

She can't hurt you, her mother's voice whispered in her ear.

She would touch the tree, and the girl wouldn't show up. That's how it would go down.

She can't terrorize me forever. And what's the worst she could do to me?

Kill me.

She's just a spirit. She can't hurt you.

Her mom had reassured her many times of that fact after finding out about Emmie's gift.

Emmie tensed as she stretched her arm out further and moved closer to the tree. Her feet crunched through dried leaves and twigs.

The Hanging Girl *must* have moved on. She didn't appear. The tree's gray and brown lumpy bark rippled across its surface like a layer of dead skin. She wanted to touch its carcass. She leaned in during the last step and scraped the tips of her fingers across the cool and coarse bark.

Feels like death.

She clenched her teeth and dug her fingers into the tree, breaking off a piece of the bark. She squeezed it in her hand, staring at the bare spot of the tree she'd exposed.

"I'll chop you down myself if I have to."

She dropped the piece of bark on the ground and then walked under the branch where the Hanging Girl had hung. She stared up at the underside of the branch. A coolness passed around her.

"I'm not scared of you anymore."

The chill enveloped her until she stepped out again from under the tree.

"I win." She clutched her hands into fists, then walked toward the house. "I win!"

She didn't look back. A sense of freedom rushed through her, but also a crawling along the back of her neck. An icy finger daring her to turn around.

❧ 17 ❧

The next morning she checked the bucket of water under the leak. Half full. She sighed and lugged it to the bathroom to pour out into the toilet. No more water leaking from the ceiling, but she returned the bucket to her room and placed it in the same location, just in case.

After a sluggish Saturday-morning routine, she plodded downstairs, still brushing her hair.

Someone's car rumbled outside. Emmie rushed to the windows, peering out at a white minivan in the driveway. A woman with purple hair sat in the driver's seat.

"Sarah." Emmie's mood jumped, and she smiled. She raced to the front door and flung it open.

Sarah waved as she climbed out of her car carrying two cups of coffee. "Are you still painting this morning?"

Emmie eyed the coffee. "That's the plan."

Sarah strolled up the sidewalk. "One of these is for you, by the way."

"You're amazing."

Sarah gazed at Emmie. "Someone didn't sleep well last night."

"Can you tell?"

"It's in your eyes." Sarah stepped up to the door and handed one of the cups to Emmie. "I've seen that look in nurses who've worked extra-long hours."

"The storm kept me up. Come in." Emmie breathed in the coffee's sweet aroma while moving out of the way for Sarah. A caramel frappé, she believed. How sweet in every way... "The others will be here soon."

Sarah wore torn blue jeans and a grungy blue shirt. She moved in closer. "Anything else on your mind?"

"Always." Emmie laughed. "I'm fine."

"Did something happen last night that made you not sleep?"

Emmie shrugged. "Just a typical night. I knew what I was getting into when I moved back in here."

"Meaning?"

"The girl. You know."

"The ghost? You saw her last night?"

"I think I did. Or something, anyway."

"Can't you tell her to just... go?"

"Don't you think I've tried?" Emmie thought of her incursion into the back yard the night before.

"What about getting a priest?" Sarah asked. "Do an exorcism?"

"This isn't a demon possession, just a haunting. I doubt a priest could help. I'm hoping things have changed since I left. Maybe it'll be better since the house was empty for a while. Maybe the girl moved on."

"You said you saw something. What if she hasn't?"

Someone rang the doorbell. Emmie pressed her lips together. Maybe it was better that they should stop talking about it. She walked over and swung the door open. John paused on the sidewalk, posing with his chin up, a paint brush in each hand, and wearing white painter overalls already dabbed with streaks of green and brown.

"You look *so* different in those clothes." Emmie laughed.

John walked up the steps, nodding. "You don't like it?"

They hugged at the door and she led him inside to the living room. "I like anything you wear as long as I can just relax on the couch with my coffee while you finish up." She walked toward the couch.

"Get back here," John growled.

Emmie turned with a grin and walked back, gesturing toward Sarah. "This is a friend from high school—Sarah."

John shook her hand. "Nice to meet you."

Emmie put her hand on Sarah's shoulder. "She offered to help this morning, so of course I took her up on it."

"Love the hair."

"I'm a nurse." Sarah grinned.

"That explains it."

Sarah clasped her hands. "You probably don't remember me, but we met once before—not under the best of circumstances. You pulled me over for speeding a long time ago."

John cringed. "Were you speeding?"

"Yes."

He nodded. "Okay then. I hope that won't stop us from working together today."

Sarah chuckled. "It won't. I was a wild teenager when it happened."

"I never hold a grudge. Life's too short." He stared down at Emmie's clothes. "Anything else you can wear? You're going to get paint all over them."

"I should probably put on some ratty clothes," Emmie said. "Who am I kidding? That describes most of my wardrobe. Give me a few minutes and I'll be ready."

Emmie ran upstairs and dressed into an old pair of shorts and a t-shirt. By the time she ran back downstairs, John and Sarah had already set up the painting tarps over the floor.

Mary had also arrived, standing in the living room in sweatpants and a dark red shirt.

"Good morning, Emmie," Mary said. "Are you ready to join our adventure?"

"Absolutely. Thanks for helping me." Emmie gestured to Sarah. "This is Sarah."

"We've met. I knew Sarah and her family before they moved away. Same church for a while, but I stopped attending..."

Mary didn't finish the sentence, but Emmie understood. ... *after Frankie was gone.* Mary had a strange politeness sometimes.

John stared at the far wall in the living room. "We have a little work ahead of us. Stripping off the wallpaper has been the hardest part so far. Painting will be a snap."

"I can help with that," Sarah said. "I know a trick to remove the wallpaper."

"Heaven sent. I'll be right back." John walked out to his truck.

He returned with a five-gallon bucket of tools and an armful of paint tarps and brought them through the house to Mary's old apartment. The others followed John's lead.

Emmie watched Mary's face as they entered her old apartment, ready to escort her out or comfort her if it seemed like too much. *The weight of Frankie's memory must feel awful now.* Emmie couldn't even imagine what Mary must be going through.

"If you gals can spread out the tarps across the floor, I'll go back and grab the ladder from my truck after we're set up."

"Got it." Sarah scooped up both tarps before Emmie could say anything and walked through the double doors leading to Mary's apartment. The doors faced each other between the two separate areas of the house, and either side could lock them for privacy.

Emmie followed her.

"It's about time this place got a makeover." Mary gave a too bright grin, but her eyes had reddened and drooped.

Emmie walked to the door and opened it. Stale air passed over her, and within that, a familiar scent of forgotten memories. The blinds were closed, but stark beams of sunlight streamed in through the cracks.

"Not many people have been back here since you left," Emmie said.

Everything looked the same as she remembered, but all the wonderful things Mary had done to make it warm and welcoming were gone. The old wallpaper was an intricate flower design, the colors reminiscent of the 1950s, but she didn't remember seeing it before, maybe because Mary had adorned all the walls with pictures and artwork.

Sarah gasped. "What happened there?"

Emmie followed Sarah's gaze to the ceiling. Someone had gouged a number deep into the ceiling below Emmie's bedroom.

6

❧ 18 ❧

White particles and chunks of plaster lay sprinkled over the floor below the etched number.

"Looks like someone left you some graffiti," Sarah said.

Emmie's eyes widened. "That wasn't there when I moved out."

"You think someone broke in?" Mary asked.

John hurried over to the back door and checked the deadbolt. "Locked." He walked around the room checking the windows. "Weird. Anyone else have a key to get in here?"

"Just you and me, John." Emmie's breath slowed as she scrutinized the cuts in the ceiling.

"Why the number six?" Sarah asked.

"No idea." Emmie opened the blinds over the windows facing out into the backyard. The room's light spilled out across the grass below, and behind the garage the top branches of the oak tree stood silhouetted against the blue sky. Bug Eyes.

You did this, didn't you?

"Should we call the police?" Sarah asked.

"Hello," John said. "You've got the best cop in town right here."

Sarah laughed. "Oh, sorry, I forgot."

"I don't see any sign of a forced entry." He peered around. "No footprints. It has been a few months since I've checked back here. Probably some teens found a way in during summer break. We'll have the locks changed, just to be sure."

"Do you have a broom, Emmie?" Mary asked.

Emmie glanced up at the 6 again and shook her head. "I didn't bring one."

How would they get that *out of the ceiling?* It was as if the Hanging Girl were branding her house like cattle. But the number made no sense.

"I've got a broom in my truck." John walked out toward the front door. "I'll grab that ladder now too."

Mary put her arm over Emmie's shoulders. "Don't let it bother you. We'll get it all back to normal soon."

Back to normal.

She'd never known normal in her entire life. But she nodded and walked over to the first bedroom, Mary's old room. "These are smaller than I remember."

"They were okay for what we needed back then," Mary said, "but it helped that your parents allowed Frankie to run free in the house. He would have gone mad being cooped up in his room all winter."

Emmie passed by the single small bathroom between the two rooms. Just a toilet and a sink. She moved on to look inside Frankie's room. The same size and look as Mary's room, except for the visible signs that a child had once inhabited that space. Drawings and illegible words mixed in with the flowers of the wallpaper. Dozens of small stickers dotted the walls, mainly from old cartoons and popular children's books Frankie had collected while staying there.

Mary looked at Emmie. "It was wonderful living with you and your parents while I was single with Frankie, even though it was such a small space. I was lonely back then, but we were happy, and I wish Frankie could have seen the farm and lived there."

"Me too." Emmie put her arm around Mary and pulled her closer.

Sarah approached the window to the backyard. "At least the kids had space to run back there."

Emmie walked over and stood next to her. The Hanging Tree towered over the garage. The nearest neighbor in that direction was beyond a narrow field, separated by a small forest. "Frankie and I used to watch the farmer plow that field when we were kids. That was our entertainment back then."

Sarah laughed. "The kids nowadays can't be bothered to look away from their phones."

Mary stepped up beside Emmie. "Lots of memories in this place," she muttered.

The Hanging Tree branches swayed.

Without waiting for Emmie to say anything, Mary stepped over to the wall next to the door and ripped away a loose corner of wallpaper. "I never liked that color. Let's make a mess."

Emmie chuckled. "That's the spirit."

Mary ripped down another large section of wallpaper, bundled it up into a ball, and hurled it at Emmie. "It's just like therapy."

Emmie tore at a different section. "Maybe this won't take all day." She tore off smaller strips, digging in her fingernails to separate it from the wall, until some larger sections refused to peel away. "Or not."

Mary struggled with a large strip. "I spoke too soon. This is a little more difficult to remove than the living room."

"Whoever put this up, used too much glue," Sarah said. "There's a better way to take it down. I brought some special wallpaper remover in my car. I'll be right back."

Mary and Emmie stood side by side, clawing away as much as they could while waiting for John and Sarah to return, throwing the scraps into the center of the room.

"It's never easy making changes," Mary said, "but after all the mess I think you'll find it was worth the trouble."

"I hope so. This house has weighed me down for too long."

John returned a short time later with a step ladder and the broom, placing them in the center of the room.

Sarah followed him with a bucket, two spray bottles, and other tools. "The older plaster walls are always a problem, but this will work magic." She mixed a solution in the bucket and they sprayed down all the difficult areas. Within thirty minutes, it was done, and shredded wallpaper covered the floor.

"That was more difficult than I expected," Emmie said.

"The living room wasn't this hard," John said. "The previous owners really stuck it on good, unfortunately for us."

When they finished ripping down wallpaper in the central area of Mary's old apartment, Emmie and Sarah moved into Frankie's old room, while John and Mary laid down tarps to paint.

Emmie went to the corner of the room where Frankie's bed had sat. An area of the wall was sunk in near the floor, and a circular section of the wallpaper didn't match the rest, angling at 45 degrees against the surrounding vertical patterns. It looked like someone had kicked in that part of the wall—probably Frankie—and then attempted to patch it up. She squatted to get a closer look.

"Did you patch the wall down here, Mary?" Emmie asked.

Mary walked into the room and looked. "Not that I know of."

Emmie started peeling away the wallpaper from that area, but the circular section popped out, revealing a hole. "I didn't know this was here."

"I didn't either." Mary leaned in closer.

"Do you think Frankie cut into the wall? Why would he do that?"

"I don't think so..."

Emmie crouched lower to peer into the hole. "The insulation is missing. All I see is the backside of the outer wall."

Mary leaned in. "I guess that would explain why it was so cold in here."

"We can patch that up," John said over Emmie's shoulder.

Mary dug out her cellphone and moved closer, using her cellphone in flashlight mode to peer inside the hole. "Let's see what's in there." Before Emmie could say anything, Mary stretched her hand inside the hole, reaching a few inches into the darkness before screeching and pulling her arm back out. "Oh my God!"

"What's wrong?" Emmie asked.

"Something bit me."

"Cover the hole," John urged.

Emmie plugged the hole again with the piece she had pulled out. "Are you okay?"

Mary nursed her finger. Blood dripped onto the painting tarp. "Something moved in there. Maybe a rat."

"Did you see it?"

"No, but something bit me." Mary lifted her bloody index finger.

"I'm a nurse. Let me." Sarah examined the finger for a moment. "This doesn't look good."

John grabbed a clean rag from a bucket of painting tools and gave it to Mary. "You better go see a doctor."

"I can drive you there, Mary," Emmie said.

"I'll take her." John put his hand on her back. "She'll be fine."

Mary wrapped her finger with the rag. "You think I'll need rabies shots?"

"I'm not sure. Maybe you just pricked your finger on a nail," Sarah said. "Did you get a tetanus shot lately?"

"I think so." Mary turned to Emmie. "Sorry for ruining your painting party, Emmie."

"Don't worry about me." Emmie caressed her shoulder. "I'm just sorry you got hurt in this crappy old house."

"If it's a rat, we'll get rid of it," John said.

Emmie and Sarah walked with Mary and John to the front door.

"I'll be back as soon as I can," Mary said bravely.

"Don't worry, Mary. We can finish another day."

John left with her. Emmie and Sarah returned to Frankie's room and continued pulling down the wallpaper on a different wall.

An hour later they'd removed most of the wallpaper, leaving only one closet unfinished and the cap over the hole.

Emmie's cellphone rang. It was John.

"Hi Emmie. I'm at the doctor's office with Mary now. She's okay, but she might be here for another hour or so. She's getting a couple of stitches, and Robert is on his way. Unfortunately, whatever cut her finger went in pretty deep. The doctor didn't think it was an animal, but we need to make sure that opening is sealed up. We should have the house checked for rodents too. It's been vacant a long time. Plenty of time for small critters to make themselves at home in there."

"Tell Mary I'm so sorry it happened."

"Nobody blames you, but I'm afraid we'll need to postpone the painting."

"Of course. I wouldn't expect her to come back."

Emmie ended the call. She told Sarah what John had said.

"I'm glad she's okay, poor thing."

As she spoke, Emmie returned to the plugged hole with her cellphone and switched on the flashlight mode before crouching down in front of it.

"What are you doing?" Sarah asked. "You're not going to open it up again, are you?"

"I just want to get a good look in there. I think I saw something down near the bottom."

Emmie opened the hole.

"Probably a dead rat. I wouldn't do that if I were you. Learn from Mary's mistake."

Emmie ignored Sarah and angled her phone to see better

near the bottom of the hole. She peered into the hollow wall in all directions. Nothing inside like a rat or nails. But an object sat several inches down in the darkness, covered in dust. She reached in and grabbed something rectangular.

She pulled it out and blew off the dust. "Oh, this is interesting."

"What's that?" Sarah asked.

"A pack of tarot cards."

❧ 19 ❧

They sat in the kitchen with drinks as Emmie flipped through the cards.

"Probably the ones Frankie got from my parents. I bet he stashed them in the hole after Mary told him to get rid of them. We used to play with them a lot."

She recognized all the cards, though she hadn't seen them in such a long time. One was missing—The Tower. The card she'd found earlier in her bedroom.

"I never understood tarot cards," Sarah said. "What's that all about?"

"Well, I'm not saying I believe in them, but the idea is that you choose certain cards and a psychic will read them and predict your future. My parents were very much into it, and they encouraged me to study them. I didn't pay much attention. Frankie and I used to play with them like they were toys."

Sarah reached out, turning a couple of cards around to see them better. "Did you ever try to predict your future with them?"

"No, I never used them like that. I found them useful in a different way, though. If I focused on The Tower card, I could attract the Hanging Girl's attention." Emmie laughed. "Crazy, huh?"

"You mean she'd show up? Right in front of you?"

"Unfortunately, yes. It only happened twice. The first time was an accident, and the second time because Frankie didn't believe me. After that, I was too freaked out to do it ever again, so I took The Tower card out of the deck and threw it away somewhere. Funny thing is, I found it in my room last night, so I guess I have a full deck again. Lucky me."

"Do you think it still works?"

"What still works?"

"Communicating with the Hanging Girl."

"She's not somebody I really want to talk to."

"Maybe it'd be worth a try again."

"What for?"

"Maybe you could help her. If she's still here, I mean."

Emmie shook her head and looked into her glass, watching the ice melting as it made a cracking noise. "I told you, this doesn't really work like an exorcism. I can't help them, especially not her. If you saw her face..."

"Sorry." Sarah shrugged. "Just an idea."

Emmie took a dish rag and wiped the pack of tarot cards. They'd survived in that hole for nineteen years. Her next thoughts surprised even her.

It would be crazy to summon the Hanging Girl.

But what if I did?

Emmie stood, walked to the window and stared out into the backyard. The noon sun dissipated the nightmarish shadows she remembered from her youth, and the Hanging Tree was within view above the garage. She had confronted the tree, but not the girl. How much longer would she put up with a ghost's nightly games? She could blame the plumbing all she wanted, but she knew the truth. The shadows and noises and disturbances would get worse, just as they had while she was growing up in that house.

Maybe forcing Bug Eyes to appear would end it. She was older now, wiser and stronger. She could put up with it and live in fear during her stay or she could confront the girl.

"Maybe you're right." Emmie gazed back at Sarah, who was watching her. "And I know just how to do it."

Sarah's eyes widened. "You're going to communicate with her? Now?"

"*Meditate and communicate*, my Mom used to say." Emmie moved back to the table and looked at the cover on the pack of tarot cards. The Magician. "Yes."

"Don't you need it to be nighttime? Or during a full moon, or something like that?"

"No. That's nonsense. This girl shows up whenever the hell she wants. I mean, yeah, she's *stronger* at night, but maybe that's good for us—or me, depending on if you want to stick around to see it."

No answer from Sarah. Emmie waited.

Come on, didn't you want to know about spirits?

As if reading Emmie's mind, Sarah said firmly, "Yes, I want to stay. I want to see this."

"All right, but no guarantee she'll appear. We'll go into the basement and do it there."

Standing, Sarah looked through the window. "Why not out by the tree in the backyard? Isn't that where she was hanged?"

"She's too strong there. I'd feel better in the basement."

Sarah nodded. "Okay."

"I'll be right back."

Emmie walked into her living room and stomped up to her bedroom. She found The Tower card and added it to the tarot deck. Her footsteps echoed through the house as she descended the stairs. Sarah met her at the bottom.

"I want you to record it for me too." Emmie took out her cellphone and handed it to Sarah.

"All right. Should I be ready to call 911?"

"You should be prepared for anything with this girl."

"Is she dangerous?"

Emmie shook her head. "She's never touched me. But..."

Sarah nodded slowly. "I understand. And why record it?"

"For a friend. Well, not really a friend, just a guy I met. He's looking for proof of the afterlife. Maybe I can kill two birds with one stone."

Cutting through the kitchen, Emmie grabbed a metal folding chair, then led Sarah down into the basement, stopping in an open area and keeping the lights on. The musty smell and cool air reminded Emmie again of playing down there as a kid with her parents nearby. No protection now if something went wrong. She was a big girl. She could handle it.

Emmie sat on the chair, her bare lower legs pressing against the cold metal.

"Where do you want me to stand?" Sarah asked.

"Right there." Emmie pointed.

Sarah positioned herself in front of Emmie.

Emmie opened the pack of tarot cards and pulled out The Tower. She held it face up in her right palm so she could see it, focus on it, and she cupped her left palm under her right.

"Okay, start recording," Emmie said.

Sarah nodded.

Emmie focused on the flames of the tower and the two falling figures. Her eyelids fluttered and almost closed, but all the time she kept the card visible at the bottom of her sight. The lightning, the smoke, the fire, and the falling figures shifted on the card as she stared. The scene came to life like an early cartoon.

Now the scene transformed from a cartoon to real life. The horror played out in the little card as the tower transformed into the Hanging Tree. One falling figure became the Hanging Girl, falling from her rope, slowly dropping, until...

Snap. The rope caught her neck and jerked her body sideways. Her mouth lurched open as if to scream. No sound escaped her as her tongue drooped out. A strained, horrible grin froze on her face. Her eyes wide and white, she turned her gaze to Emmie.

Emmie's heart beat faster. A cool air rushed across her skin as if she were standing in front of an air conditioner. She shivered and watched the card.

The Hanging Girl grabbed the rope above her neck without changing her expression. Lifting herself out of the noose, she dropped to the ground, her nightgown waving and crumpling beneath her when she hit it. She sank below the edge of the card.

"She's coming." Emmie swallowed.

The door leading into Mary's apartment opened and slammed shut. No way to avoid it now.

"Are you okay?" Sarah asked.

"Yes, for now."

Footsteps creaked across the basement's ceiling, crossing through Mary's apartment, her living room and kitchen.

Within the darkness, a gurgling sound filled the air. Just a faint whisper at first, like some clogged sink bubbling as the air escaped. It grew louder, and a groan came from somewhere nearby.

Still focused on the card at her chest, Emmie saw a figure appear at the edge of her vision. She opened her eyes wide and faced the spirit.

It was a smaller shadowy spirit standing a few feet away, choking and gurgling. Not the Hanging Girl. This spirit faded in and out, shifting between forms, until it settled into its true identity.

The sight both terrified and surprised her.

Frankie stood gasping for air, with his arms out toward Emmie.

❦ 20 ❧

"**M**y God, Frankie, is that you?" Emmie cried. She couldn't get up, or she might lose him.

No sound from the spirit, but Frankie's arms kept reaching out toward her. She tried to grab hold of his hands, but instead she swiped through his spirit form. Another puff of cold air chilled her skin. He wasn't solid flesh, as ghosts sometimes were, or a barely visible cloud like a traditional spirit; Frankie wavered somewhere between the two. His form faded and then solidified.

A barrier stood between them, churning; it was like gazing through melting glass. His mouth hung open, forming intelligible, silent words. His wide eyes stared at her, and he gargled out noises that chilled her blood. Not a single word came out clearly, as if he were talking through a layer of water.

Emmie tried to make sense of the vision and struggled to understand what Frankie was saying. She intensified her focus on him, but now she sensed other spirits approaching.

She knew one thing—if she was seeing him, he hadn't died in an accident. And he would never have killed himself. Emmie squeezed the tarot card between her fingers as she voiced the only horrible possibility.

"Frankie, who did this to you? Who killed you?"

His mouth opened and closed, and the watery gargling came through.

More spirits entered Emmie's awareness. The channel she'd opened to confront the Hanging Girl needed to close soon or more would crowd in around her, begging for help. It would become unbearable. But she wouldn't close it now, with Frankie in front of her.

"Frankie, can you move toward me?" Emmie pleaded.

Frankie's spirit floated closer as she intensified her concentration on him, but another spirit appeared alongside him. A lost boy a little older than Frankie, wearing the decades-old school uniform. His body was more transparent than Frankie's, but the physical violence on him was clear. She avoided looking directly at the other boy, instead increasing her focus on Frankie.

The door at the top of the basement stairs opened and slammed shut. Emmie dropped the tarot card. Footsteps stomped down the stairs. She shivered. Distinct footsteps from a barefoot teenage girl. The Hanging Girl.

Emmie's eyes teared up as she tried to grasp Frankie. For a moment he solidified, and her skin bristled at the sensation of his energy passing through her. He still looked the same after all these years. His sweet face stared at her longingly. His small frame and frail posture reminded her of the way she had found his body near the edge of the lake.

"Who did this to you?" she insisted.

Frankie continued to communicate, opening and closing his mouth, but only watery gurgles came through.

The Hanging Girl reached the bottom of the stairs. The hair on the back of Emmie's neck stood. Only a few feet away now. The girl's feet slapped against the cold concrete floor, moving toward her. She wouldn't look away from Frankie. The Hanging Girl's strained, forced whisper moved in closer to her ear.

Emmie's body chilled as an icy pressure tingled her shoulder.

She can't hurt me.

"Look at me!" the Hanging Girl screamed.

Still, Emmie ignored her. "Frankie, I don't have long. The others will pull me away from you. Say the person's name!"

The Hanging Girl moved in behind Emmie. A freezing sensation crept up the side of her neck. The girl's fingers—scraping like icicles across her skin—stopped at the edge of her hair. Then the girl yanked a handful back. Pain tore across Emmie's scalp as her face swung up and to the right. The girl's mouth moved in closer to her left ear.

"What are you doing in my house?" the girl screeched. "Get out of my house!"

Throwing her arms back, Emmie tried to push the Hanging Girl out of the way as Frankie strained forward to speak. The girl let out a guttural groan like gas escaping from a pipe.

Emmie turned her face toward the Hanging Girl but refused to meet her eyes. "Go away!"

"This is my house. Mine."

"It's not yours anymore. You're dead. Go away."

"Liar!"

A wind rushed through the basement as if a tornado had touched down.

The girl pulled Emmie's hair, then thrust her further sideways. Emmie toppled off the chair, stopping only inches from cracking her head against the cement floor. Frankie stayed with her, maneuvering between the two spirits that crowded in front of Emmie. The older boy pleaded in silence beside Frankie, his distorted face white and bloated.

Two more spirits appeared from the darkness, reaching out for Emmie, one holding a stuffed animal and the other limping in pain as if some violent impact had killed him. Their voices came through as screams and cries, drowning out Frankie's attempts to communicate.

The Hanging Girl still held Emmie in her grip. She yanked her hair again, this time forcing Emmie's face toward her.

"Frankie, say the name." Emmie moved as close as she could to Frankie and listened to every tortured breath for even a single word. Something that might provide a clue to his death.

With her eyes focused on Frankie's mouth, a gurgled word came through. Other voices in the room drowned out the sound, but the word on his lips was clear. *Bobby.*

Frankie repeated it again.

"Bobby," Emmie whispered.

"Get out of my house!" the Hanging Girl screamed in her ear.

Emmie stiffened and looked straight into the girl's face. The girl's bulging bug eyes and gaping mouth hovered inches away. Nausea spread through Emmie's stomach. Every muscle in her body screamed for her to run as she had during every other confrontation with Bug Eyes. She clenched her fists as if to bat the spirit away. "You're dead. This is my house now. It's not yours anymore."

"It's my house. You stole it from me."

"Go away! Go to the light, or just anywhere. Go back to hell!"

The Hanging Girl tightened her grip on Emmie's hair and pulled harder.

Emmie cringed and cried out, focusing again on Frankie. The other spirits crowded in around him, blocking most of his energy. All of them reached out toward her with pleading arms and sorrowful, pained faces. "I can't help any of you. Don't you understand that? I don't know what to do. Please leave me alone. I just want to help my friend."

The Hanging Girl slipped her hands down and clutched Emmie's neck. Her fingertips dug into Emmie's throat. "You'll hang for this."

Emmie gasped for breath.

Sarah's panicked voice cried out from a few feet away, "Are you okay? Emmie?"

How was the Hanging Girl choking her now? The words of her Mom flashed through her mind: *They can't hurt you.*

Yes, they can. It hurts, Mom.

Emmie stopped breathing. The Hanging Girl's grip around her throat tightened. She clawed at the spirit's wrists. Nothing to grab. She swung her arms in the air and twisted away. She heaved in a deep breath and coughed. The Hanging Girl stood over her as she lay gasping on the ground. "Now..." she coughed, "... I lay me down to sleep..."

The Hanging Girl sneered, but moved closer again, her hands curled into claws stretching out toward Emmie's neck

"... I pray the Lord my soul to keep."

I'm going to die.

No more time to communicate with Frankie. She swatted at the invisible hands closing around her neck.

Again, "Now I lay me down to sleep, I pray the Lord my soul to keep."

The Hanging Girl's fingers touched Emmie's cheek before stopping.

Emmie repeated the line again, faster this time.

Go away.

"Emmie, please stop," Sarah said, "you're scaring me."

Emmie focused on Sarah now, staring up at the cellphone and her panicked face.

Frankie's spirit faded behind the others.

The Hanging Girl's hands passed through Emmie, freezing her skin and sending shivers into her chest and neck.

They can't hurt you.

Hell if they can't, Mom.

The other spirits moved away and disappeared. The Hanging Girl remained, batting her arms at Emmie until she, too, disappeared from sight.

Emmie nursed her neck as Sarah stepped closer, occupying the same space the Hanging Girl had only moments earlier.

"Do you want me to call an ambulance?" Sarah asked.

"I'm okay," Emmie moaned.

Sarah held her arm as she struggled to stand. "You don't sound okay."

Leaning forward onto Sarah's shoulder, Emmie covered her face as she cried. The scene played over in her mind. *Poor Frankie. What a horrible mess.*

Bobby.

✿ 21 ✿

Sarah's face warmed, and yet she shivered. The cool basement air rushed across her face, but something else deep inside her burned as if a flash of fire had ripped through her. She *felt* a spirit's presence, yet it was a far different sensation from the gentle elation of a soul freeing itself from a ravaged body as it passed away. Now, it was all bitterness and a sickening intensity. Something was horribly wrong.

Emmie's eyes were wide and wet. Her head sagged, and she hunched forward. Whatever that poor girl saw had more than just shaken her up. It had taken hold of her spirit and affected her on a deep level.

Sarah reached out toward her, but Emmie was still panting and crying, staring into the empty air in front of her.

"Emmie?" Sarah asked. "How are you doing? This doesn't feel right. I think you should get to a doctor."

Emmie's hands trembled as she wiped away the tears. "No, just give me a minute."

Pipes rattled and clanked from the other side of the stairs.

Emmie's neck was red. Her flesh had compressed and stretched during the recording, shifting and tightening as if something unseen had held her. Any other nurse would have concluded Emmie was having a seizure.

Sarah looked into her eyes. "Can you breathe now?"

"They were here. She grabbed me."

"They? You saw more than one?"

"You didn't see them?" Emmie said with disappointment. "The Hanging Girl showed up, but also Frankie, and some others. You must have seen something?"

"I did." Sarah scrubbed backward through the video, then turned the cellphone's screen toward Emmie and stepped closer. "Lots of shadows around you. See there?" Sarah pointed and stopped on a frame.

Emmie stared into the screen as the recording played back a section. Her breathing slowed. "We captured some of it."

Sarah nodded. "Something's there, *definitely* there, but nothing physical. It was so strange. The entire time I had this horrible feeling, like when a violent patient needs to be sedated. Not like anything I normally feel when someone passes away at the hospital."

Emmie stared into Sarah's eyes. "You believe me, right? Even if you didn't see anything physical?"

"Yes. No doubt in my mind. It was overwhelming, to say the least." Sarah eyed the empty corners of the room. "How many of them appeared to you?"

"Five or six. When I opened up the communication, other spirits moved in to talk."

"I think they're still here." Sarah closed her mouth and swallowed. "My chest is... vibrating, like a burst of radiation or I'm getting a low voltage shock."

"That's her." Emmie looked back at the screen. "Play the video from the beginning."

Sarah eyed Emmie. "I think we should go upstairs. We'll watch everything up there together. I'm worried about you. You're sweating, but it's freezing down here."

Emmie wiped her forehead and cheeks. "I don't feel so good."

"You're *not* good." Sarah placed her palm on Emmie's forehead. *Like a high fever.* "You're burning up. Take my arm. This space isn't good for either of us."

Sarah helped Emmie stand again just as the lights flickered and went out. Sarah gasped and held back a scream. The cellphone's screen, still frozen on the one frame of Emmie surrounded by a flurry of shadows, blinded her for a moment as everything around her went dark. "Emmie?"

"I'm fine. This happens all the time."

Sarah held up the cellphone screen, lighting their way toward the exit.

Emmie staggered alongside her over to the bottom of the stairs. "Don't worry. She's just trying to scare us."

Sarah shuddered. "I didn't think it would be so intense."

"Are you sorry you came?"

"No, but I still have that sick feeling in my stomach, like someone is here."

"That's her."

"She turned off the lights?" Sarah asked.

"She tripped the breaker, I'm sure of it. It's been like that as far back as I can remember."

Emmie wobbled like someone who'd just awakened from a deep sleep. Sarah put her arm around Emmie's back. "Let me help you up the stairs."

"I'll turn on the lights first." Emmie veered toward the laundry room. "The circuit panel is back here. It'll just take a minute."

Panic welled up inside Sarah's chest. Behind her—scratching, like someone's fingernails across the brick wall. Emmie wasn't moving fast enough. Sarah pushed in closer. The hair on the back of her neck bristled. No sign of the sound's source—her imagination filled in the gaps.

Sarah held up the cellphone as Emmie opened the circuit

panel and flipped a switch. The lights popped on again. A flood of relief passed through Sarah, but the blazing emotions of an unseen force still surged through her chest.

"I can still feel her." Sarah switched off the cellphone.

Emmie nodded sympathetically. "She's getting stronger."

Under the laundry room's unshielded harsh light, the patches of redness across Emmie's neck looked worse than Sarah had imagined. She pulled back the collar of Emmie's shirt and wiped away the damp locks of hair. "Do you have any medical supplies here?"

"Not much. Am I bleeding?"

"I don't think so, but we should at least get some ice on that."

Emmie rubbed her neck. "She's never gotten that close to me before."

They walked upstairs and Emmie sat at the table holding her head in her hands with her eyes closed.

At the refrigerator, Sarah dug out several ice cubes from a tray in the freezer, wrapping them in a paper towel before bringing them over to Emmie. "Hold this on your neck. The right side is a little worse than the left. It should keep the swelling down. I still think you might want to see a doctor, but I guess you already have a top notch nurse here now, right?"

Emmie smiled warmly. "I'm glad you're here."

"I'm glad I got to share this with you."

"Let's watch it." Emmie gestured to the cellphone.

Sarah turned on the cellphone's screen. The glare from the window nearby wasn't helping, but not much she could do. She closed the blind and sat next to Emmie holding the cellphone between them. She started the recording from the beginning.

The noises and shadows played as they stared into the screen without saying a word. It was all there as Sarah had watched it play out a short time earlier. The inner burning and intensity flooded back as she relived the scene in her mind.

Emmie moved the ice pack from one side to the other as the

scene progressed. Halfway through the recording, she broke into tears.

Sarah looked into her eyes. "You want me to stop the video?"

Emmie shook her head. "I'm okay."

The refrigerator rumbled to life as something thumped against the floor beneath Sarah's feet. She jumped, though Emmie seemed not to notice.

Another thump against the floor. Sarah paused her breath and listened. Something circled in the air, a bristling like an electric field. It rushed through her chest. The kitchen cooled, then warmed again. Emmie glanced up for a moment, squinting into the empty air across the kitchen, then stared back down at the video.

"Did you feel that?" Sarah asked.

"Yes. A child's spirit. Not the Hanging Girl or Frankie. He'll move on soon, as long as I don't focus on him. They always do."

Sarah watched Emmie's face. *Dear God, how can you be so calm with everything that's happened?*

The video continued with Sarah scrutinizing the motion of the shadows around Emmie. Were those hands around Emmie's neck? And the faint outline of a figure, almost imperceptibly, hovering nearby?

The recording ended a few minutes later and dried tears left trails down Emmie's cheeks. They sat in silence for a few seconds before Emmie spoke up. "Frankie kept saying the name Bobby."

"Who's Bobby?" Sarah said softly.

"I think he meant Bobby Norris. When I was little, they kept me away from too much information around Frankie's death and said it was an accident. But in the library I read more about it, and this guy's name was in an article. He was the swimming coach that taught the kids at the lake."

"We should go to the police."

Emmie shook her head. "John will listen to me, but showing him the video won't do any good. He's never said so, but I know he thinks this is all nonsense. I want that ghost hunter to see it first. I wonder what he'll say about it."

"What difference does it matter what he thinks? *I* believe you, Emmie. I saw it too, and I *felt* it. That's more important than seeing."

"I know, but I just want to get his opinion."

"You don't need his validation."

"Probably not, but I think it would help me, in a way. Nobody's looked at this from a scientific perspective. We both know it's real, but... I've never considered myself to be..."

"Normal?"

"That, and... sane. Maybe someone can prove all this some day, connect the paranormal as a real part of science. I'd love to wave a piece of verified evidence in the face of everyone who mocked me growing up."

Sarah stared at the blank screen of the cellphone. "I'm not sure that's possible."

"I'm going to let him try. Can't hurt, right?"

Sarah shrugged.

Emmie glanced toward the living room. "The only problem is that I don't have an Internet connection here at the house. I'll need to find Wi-Fi somewhere to send the file."

"We can go to my house to send it, but it's a long drive from here. Maybe the library? I know they have Wi-Fi there, but it's slow. Or Mary's cafe?"

Mary. Emmie rubbed her forehead. "Poor Mary. How can I tell her about seeing Frankie now, and that his death wasn't an accident, after all she's been through?"

"You don't need to tell her right now, do you?"

"But she's been asking about him for years, knowing about my gift. This is just going to make her misery worse."

"Wouldn't she want to know the truth?"

Emmie paused. "Maybe. But I think it's more likely to re-open an old wound." She stared at the blank screen on her cell-phone. "I can't tell her about it—not yet. Not until I know more about what happened. We'll stop by the cafe to send the file to Finn, and if she's already there, I won't say a word."

Sarah nodded once. "Whatever you think is best."

"Do you work today?"

"Not until four."

"I hope I'm not holding you back. Maybe you'd rather not stick around after all this. I certainly wouldn't blame you."

"Are you kidding me? This is all the stuff I've wondered about since my experiences in the hospital began. And, anyway, I can't leave you like this." Sarah glanced at Emmie's neck. "I'd love to help you through it."

"Thank you." Emmie smiled, then stood up. The makeshift icepack was now only a lumpy pile of wet paper towels on the table. "Okay, great. Let's get this video sent off to Finn, and then we'll find out more info on this Bobby guy."

❧ 2 2 ❧

On the drive over to Mary's cafe, Emmie made a right turn, and the sun glimmered off Sarah's purple hair.

"I'm just curious. Why did you choose purple?"

Sarah's eyes widened, and she laughed. "I just wanted to do something crazy, I guess."

"It's not crazy."

"For me, it is. I've never been the kind of person to do anything shocking. My parents haven't even seen it yet—won't they be surprised! I did it myself a couple of months ago, just to try something out of the ordinary."

"I don't remember you being the ordinary girl in high school. You always hung around with those popular girls."

Sarah winced and shook her head. "No, I was such an idiot back then. Just a shy kid trying to fit in somewhere. That was all just a big act, playing the rebellious teen, and I remember getting so excited after I'd won their *approval*." Sarah pretended to puke. "I didn't like any of them, but it doesn't matter anymore. They're all gone now—one of them died, and the rest moved away. Little good all that brown-nosing did me. So I just try to have a little fun with my life." She gestured toward her hair. "This is about as risqué as I get."

"It looks nice."

"Thanks. One thing about having colored hair is that all the patients remember me. I guess that can be good or bad, though. It either makes them smile and brightens their day, or I'm an easy target when things go wrong." Sarah imitated a grumpy patient. *"That purple-haired nurse forgot my extra fruit cup!"* Sarah chuckled. "I can't get away with anything."

Emmie laughed. "They really sound like that?"

"Oh, yeah."

Mary's cafe came into view and Emmie pulled up behind a white van on the street about half a block away. She glanced toward the cafe's front entrance. The colorful painted wood sign over the doorway invited everyone in—*Sunshine Cafe.*

Lots of families strolled along the sidewalks that afternoon, even though dark rain clouds on the horizon threatened to spoil the fun later on. Emmie scanned the faces for anyone she might know. Not a single person looked familiar. Had the town changed *that* much since she'd left?

A rusting pickup truck sped by on the street, and her car wavered in its air wake. Outside the cafe on the sidewalk, patrons filled three small tables, sipping their drinks and eating food.

Through the storefront window, Emmie spotted Natalie helping customers at the counter. Mary and Robert hadn't returned yet. *Perfect.* Better that they were gone, considering all she had seen and heard, but she hoped Mary was okay and maybe on her way home by now.

One lone table sat unoccupied at the end.

Emmie turned off the engine and glanced over at Sarah.

She was staring at Emmie's neck, then reached over and brushed back Emmie's hair. "Sorry, just seeing how you're doing. The redness is gone."

Emmie rubbed it. *Still sore.* "I've never had anything like that happen before. I'll need to be more careful next time. Things got a little... carried away this time."

Sarah nodded. "Does it hurt anywhere else?"

Emmie smiled. *Only on the inside. Only when I laugh. Only...
everywhere.* "No. I'm feeling better. Thanks."

"Can you get the Wi-Fi signal from out here? If you can, let's
sit outside." Sarah pointed to the empty table on the sidewalk.
"Get some fresh air."

"Great idea." Emmie typed the Wi-Fi code in her cellphone.
Sunshine. The signal was poor, just one bar, but it worked. "Good
enough to send the video."

They climbed out of the car and walked toward the cafe.

Sarah split off toward the entrance. "You grab the table and
I'll grab some food. You must be hungry by now. I'm buying.
They make good sandwiches here. You want one?"

The smell of baked goods filled the air and her hunger
surged. "Thanks. I'll have what you're having." Better to skip
Mary's offer for free coffee; she didn't feel like talking to Natalie
either today.

"Sounds good. I'll be right back." Sarah disappeared inside
the cafe.

Emmie set her purse on the table and sat down in one of the
black metal chairs. One patron glanced over at her, but the
others were absorbed in their cellphones and coffees.

No need to bother Finn with a phone call—easier to send a
text message. She dug out the business card he'd given her. Finn
Adams, Contributing Editor & Photojournalist. She typed his
number, attaching the video, along with a brief message—just
her name and a cryptic, *Recorded this in my basement*—and sent it.
He'd understand.

Her phone whooshed a short time later, alerting her to the
delivered message. Now, just to wait for a reaction.

Further down the sidewalk a black-haired young boy stood
alone in muddy green and navy-blue torn clothes. He stared at
Emmie with no obvious signs of trauma until he reached out to
her. One arm jutted sideways at an unnatural angle. He stumbled

forward, turning his head, and the back side of his skull came into view. Crushed in like a crescent moon.

Emmie glanced away. She had tuned her psychic senses earlier, like adjusting rabbit ear antennae to pick up an over-the-air channel, but she hadn't switched it off completely. *The price for communicating with the Hanging Girl and Frankie.* She could ignore him like every other vision, but now she gazed back at him again as he moved closer. "What do you want me to do?" she whispered. Her chest tightened. "I'll figure it out. Just give me some time."

Her cellphone rang, and she jumped. Finn's number appeared on the screen.

"Hello?" she answered before the second ring.

She looked back toward the boy, but he was gone.

"Hi Emmie. This is Finn. I got your video."

She waited a moment for him to continue, then spoke up, "What did you think?"

"Interesting stuff. Enough that I'd like to set up my equipment in your house tomorrow, if you're okay with that."

"We recorded it this morning."

"Who was with you?"

"Just my friend, Sarah. She recorded it."

"Brave girl to keep the camera from shaking."

"I agree."

"How did this come about? Were you using a Ouija board or something like that?"

"No, it started when I tried to communicate with the Hanging Girl. I just wanted to confront her. I'm so tired of her terrorizing me, but it didn't exactly go as planned. And some other spirits showed up too. One of those spirits was Frankie, or Franklin as you know him."

"The boy who drowned?"

"Yes. He was trying to tell me something, but he couldn't get through because of all the other spirits blocking him. There's just so many of them and when I open up my mind and see into the spirit world. It's just like a rush of water into my mind. It floods in and it's hard to control. The Hanging Girl showed up then, too. It got out of hand, as you can see in the video." He was silent. "What, are you thinking I'm a nut right now?"

"No," Finn said. "I don't think you're a nut. Like I said, I'm very interested. Can I stop by in the morning? Ten a.m.? I'll set up all the equipment, and we can go over any other experiences you might have had if you feel like talking about those things?"

"Yes, as long as we keep this between us, okay? I know you're a reporter or something like that."

"A contributing editor. Doesn't work the way you think. Don't worry, I'll absolutely respect your privacy."

Emmie relaxed. "All right. Then I look forward to doing this. Maybe it'll help."

"I hope so. It can't hurt, right?"

I'm not so sure. "Okay, I'll see you tomorrow morning at ten, Finn."

"Thank you, Emmie. Tomorrow."

"Bye."

Sarah returned a short time later with food and drinks.

Emmie waited until Sarah had settled back into her seat before saying, "Finn just called about the recording I sent him. Can you stop by my house a little before ten tomorrow morning?"

"Sure. What for?"

"That's when Finn will be there."

"If you're so worried about this guy, why did you invite him over?"

"I guess I'm not *worried*, but... you never know."

Sarah nodded. "I get it. We girls have to stick together, right?" She laughed. "Sure, no problem."

They ate their meals. The sun brightened and dimmed between passing clouds just as a police car drove by. John sat in the driver's seat. No passengers. "There he goes. I guess he must have taken Mary home. I hope she's okay."

Sarah turned and followed Emmie's gaze, craning her head back. "I'm sure she's fine."

"I want to see John after this. He would know more about Bobby. Do you have time to go with me?"

Sarah checked her cellphone. "Yes, plenty of—" Her phone rang while still in her hand. "This isn't good." She frowned, then answered the call.

Judging from Sarah's face, Emmie would be going to see John on her own. Sarah gazed at the half-eaten sandwich on the plate in front of her with a scowl.

Mid-way through the call, Sarah placed her hand over the phone's microphone and moved it off to the side. "They want me to come in early. I'll tell them I can't make it."

"No, it's okay. I'm sure they really need you, right?"

Sarah scoffed. "They already work me too hard."

"I don't want you to get into trouble over me. Somebody out there needs help. You should go. I'll be okay."

Sarah accepted their request with an expressionless tone and hung up. "If it wasn't such an emergency—"

"It's totally okay."

"Some big accident."

"You better go."

Sarah sighed and grabbed her purse as she stood up. Emmie stood up with her and they hugged.

Emmie spotted the dark-haired boy again from the corner of her eye. He'd moved in closer, and now more trauma had appeared on his body. A bone in his chest poked out through one of the torn sections of his shirt.

Sarah held Emmie's hands as she backed away and looked into her eyes. "Sorry I can't go with you to see John. But I'll be there early tomorrow morning to stand between you and that guy. If he tries to lay one hand on you." Sarah smirked and waved a fist.

Emmie laughed. "I'm not too worried." She glanced back. The boy was stepping closer.

Sarah leaned forward and whispered, "You should talk with him."

Emmie's brow furrowed. "Who?"

"The child back there."

Emmie glanced back at him, then gazed into Sarah's eyes. "Do you see him too?"

"No, but I sense him, and you have that look in your eyes. I can feel his sadness and desperation."

"Another time. I promise." Emmie gestured toward her car. "You need to get going."

❄ 23 ❄

Emmie walked into the police station after passing through a security door. A stocky, muscular officer met her on the other side.

He eyed Emmie's clothes. "Who are you here to see?"

"John Ratner."

He gestured with his chin to the left. "Corner office. I'll take you there."

A man of few words.

They wound through a row of cubicles, then down a short hallway to the back. John's door was wide open as he talked on the cellphone with his feet up on his desk. The guiding officer hovered behind her until John gestured for her to come in. He mouthed, *"Close the door,"* while still conversing. Emmie closed it.

John's new office was a step up from the cramped desk he'd occupied the last time she'd been there as a teenager. Visiting him long ago had been both intimidating and comforting, but she'd found refuge in talking to him about her problems back then. No other adults in her life to talk to. No pastor, no neighbors, and certainly not her parents.

After Frankie's death, he'd defended her against a swarm of accusations and "fans" who only sought to exploit her psychic powers. With her parents always encouraging her to *"meditate and communicate,"* talking to John had been an oasis from all the chaos. A lifeline to sanity.

She'd felt safe there, despite the other officers rarely returning her smiles. He'd always listened without condemnation, although she'd figured out soon after meeting him that he didn't believe any talk about ghosts or the occult. He gently redirected comments concerning spirits toward *the facts.* And that was fine with her.

The walls were full of framed photos and awards. His desk was scattered with papers and several crime thriller novels, one of them bookmarked halfway. A row of filing cabinets along the outer wall divided two windows.

After completing his call, John sat up at his desk, adjusting his thick-rimmed glasses. "I was just about to call you. Mary's doing fine. I dropped her off at her house to rest. She cut herself pretty deep—had to get several stitches."

"Several..." Emmie winced.

"Could have been worse. They figured it was a stray nail poking through the wall. At least she'd had her tetanus shot."

"I'm glad she's okay. I feel awful."

"She'll be fine."

She leaned against the cabinet, facing him, and figured that she might as well be direct. "I have a question for you. It might sound odd, but I read about a guy named Bobby Norris in connection with Frankie's death. Do you have any information about him?"

John leaned back further in his chair. "Why do you ask?"

"It's a little hard to explain."

"I see. I'm going to need a little more than this. It's an old, closed case, Emmie."

She wondered what she could say. Maybe he suspected she was having one of her paranormal hunches, in which case he might shut her down. What would make him help her?

"I never read about the case until now," she finally repeated.

"I did at the library and saw his name. I just want to know, for my own peace of mind, that they did a good job for Frankie."

He sighed, looked away, rubbed his bristly head. She hated not telling him the whole truth when he had always been her champion, but he would not help her if he thought he was humoring her intuitions.

But it worked. He stood up with a loud creak of the chair and a sideways glance. "Let's see what I can find. Bobby lives around the lake, but he was cleared for a fact. Still, if it will give you peace of mind..." He dug into filing cabinets and pulled out a thick brown folder stuffed with documents. He set it on his desk and dropped into his seat again, glancing up at Emmie with narrow eyes. "This is all the information I have about the case."

Emmie walked over and stood by his side, eyeing the folder.

John turned it so she could see inside. "Just keep this between us, though. I'm not really supposed to give out personal information about the investigation. Not professional."

"Understood."

John flipped through the pages until he came to another folder with the name Bobby Norris at the top. "This is him. You might remember him as Mr. Norris, the swimming instructor, but after Frankie's death, he quit. Don't jump to any conclusions, though. Like I said, we cleared him. He had an alibi."

"Are you sure?"

John pulled out the folder and opened it on the desk. "Absolutely. Here it is, witnesses who saw him dining with his family. People in the restaurant, waiters..." He spread the report on the table, tapping it to show his certainty.

She couldn't let this go yet. "This Bobby guy, did he have a criminal record before this incident?"

John flipped through a few more pages and stopped to read one before answering, "Nothing. Clean as a nun's behind."

Emmie laughed and cringed. "Eww."

"He had a good alibi," John insisted.

Taking the seat across from him, she asked, "But they've been known to make mistakes, right?"

John half-nodded. "Technically, the coroner's report is always an estimate. They can nail down the time to within a few hours because of rigor mortis and body temperature, but the water could mess with that a little. But more importantly, Bobby Norris had no motive. Why would he have killed Frankie?"

"Silence him to keep some awful sexual crime a secret?" she suggested.

"No evidence of that. When there's no motive and no signs of foul play, which the body didn't appear to have, then the obvious is suspected. Frankie was learning to swim in the lake. He went in when he shouldn't have, and he drowned." Again, he narrowed his eyes at her. "Is there something that prompted you to think this guy killed Frankie?"

It's all that stuff you don't want to talk about, John.

Emmie could tell him about everything that happened in her basement. All the disturbing details about what she'd seen, but it wouldn't make any difference. He'd never wanted to hear about her psychic experiences. Just the facts, and reality as it existed in his eyes. She didn't blame him.

"I guess I've just always wondered..." Emmie looked at the top paper in the stack. A long paragraph containing details about the edge of the lake where they'd found Frankie's body.

"What's that?" he asked.

"The school has an indoor pool. Why didn't the swimming instructor use that pool to teach the kids how to swim instead of the lake?"

"We went over that too. Maybe Franklin's death was partly Bobby's fault for being a nature-loving tree hugger and insisting to teach the kids at the lake. I remember he defended his decision when we questioned him. I suppose that's why Franklin went back down there to swim alone. Maybe he felt it was safe."

Emmie shook her head. "He wouldn't have gone down there alone. And I don't think Bobby's alibi is as tight as everyone thinks. Like you said, the cold water might have affected Frankie's body temperature and messed with the time of death."

"You might be right, but that's not very likely."

"Is there anything else they brought up in the investigation that looked suspicious in any way?"

"Look, Emmie." John leaned forward. "I know his death was traumatic for a lot of people, especially you and Mary, but the investigators in this case have already gone through all this. It was just an accident, a horrible tragedy."

Her eyes met John's. "I have a feeling they missed something."

He nodded sympathetically. "I understand—I do. But we can't reopen his case without something substantial."

Emmie looked down at the papers. "If you do happen to look through it again, as an exercise, just please let me know you if you find anything in there that stands out as unusual or doesn't quite make sense."

"I will." John flipped through a few more pages, then closed the file. "That's about it."

A white label on the cover caught her eye. *Bobby Norris, 6 Lakeside Drive, Green Hills, MN.*

A chill passed through her. She'd been wrong. The Hanging Girl hadn't scrawled the number in Mary's apartment—Frankie had.

6

❧ 24 ❧

L ater that afternoon, Emmie turned onto Lakeside Drive, a winding gravel road wrapping around Crane Lake. She'd traveled along that road many times throughout her childhood, sometimes in the backseat of her parents' car on their way through the countryside, and sometimes as a young teen visiting a friend. One of the nicer areas in town.

A small Lutheran church stood across the road from the lake, an old brick building that probably had been there since they formed the town. A cornfield bordered one side. A lone blonde-haired girl sat hunched forward on the steps leading to the front door, but no sign of anyone else. Another lost spirit with a story to tell. A cemetery sprawled out beyond the church and Emmie had gone there a few times in her youth to escape from the world, but the area held too much history, and the girl on the steps watched her all the time, so she'd never gone back.

She caught sight of the numbers on the mailboxes along the road's edge. 14... 12... 10... She slowed her car. 8... The next mailbox was made of wood with a large number 6 carved into the side.

Just like the number 6 carved into the ceiling of Mary's old apartment. No mistaking it, she was in the right place.

"We're here, Frankie. Now what?"

Bobby Norris's house was a small, white, single-story rambler surrounded by bushes and trees. A blue car sat in front of a two-car garage. He was home.

She couldn't just stop right there—too suspicious if she pulled over to the side of the road to go snooping. The park and beach were just ahead. She'd stop there and walk back.

A small forest separated the houses from the beach area; she passed it and pulled into the parking lot. Several cars filled the row closest to the beach. Shrieking kids in the water and families grouped on beach towels lined the water's edge. More families huddled around the picnic tables beneath a pavilion.

She parked the car and walked over on the grass, pausing for a minute as she scanned the crowd. Some people she remembered from years earlier, but most were strangers.

To her left were the forest and the lakeshore, and beyond that the place where she'd found Frankie's body. The smell of the lake drifted over her. She'd gone back there only once since his death, just to have a good cry and feel a connection with her old friend.

She looked away. On the far side of the beach to her right stood a clump of trees where she had sometimes gathered with friends to hang out and listen to music. Her friends had never understood why she wouldn't go swimming in the lake. They didn't see the boy splashing in the water out beyond the dock and the raft. His tragedy never ended, an aimless struggle to get rescued repeated like a video clip looping every few minutes.

The boy's name was Darrell Pryor. For his fifteenth birthday, he'd gone out alone on a small boat to fish while drunk. Bad choice. He'd fallen in and drowned before anyone could reach him. Emmie was there at the beach along with a small crowd when they pulled his body from the lake, his bare chest and blue jeans dripping wet. It was the first time she'd ever seen a dead person in the flesh.

Sometimes Darrell called her name while she hung out with her friends. "Emmie! Help me!"

She always ignored his cries. No way to help him.

Her friends would pressure her to go swimming with them.

"No thanks," she'd say, and they would swim out close to the boy, oblivious to the horror happening only feet away.

"Get out here, you chicken shit!" they would call.

No way. Seeing that sight from the shore was bad enough.

Darrell was out there now, screaming and slapping his hands against the surface of the water. She turned away and headed back toward Bobby Norris's house. Her feet crunched against the gravel road on her way to Lakeside Drive. The sound of Darrell's cries faded as she moved around the other side of the forest.

Within a few minutes, she passed the forest that separated Bobby Norris's property from the beach. Standing near the end of his driveway, she stared at his house yet stayed out of sight. A birdhouse the size of a small doghouse sat perched on a steel hole near his front porch. No sign of a dog. Good. A wind chime dangling from a tree branch clinked in the light breeze. Birds chirped in the surrounding trees.

She stepped toward the forest, cutting through the ditch down into the grass and dried mud, then back up the embankment. She circled behind the trees and moved into the shadows. Stray branches poked at her as the trees cloaked her.

All right, Frankie, why did you bring me to this place? What am I going to find here?

She moved in closer toward Bobby's house. The brush cracked beneath her feet as she pushed forward to get a better view. No sign of Bobby Norris.

A subtle breeze blew across her face, and the branches swayed. Zigzagging through the trees toward the water's edge, she spotted the back porch.

He was there, sitting on a lawn chair facing the lake. A book lay open in his lap and his feet were up on a small stool. No shirt, just shorts, a long gray beard, and a balding head. A large man, but more flab than muscle.

She'd seen him around town since Frankie's death, but had never felt threatened by him until now.

A shrill cry from the lake startled her. Darrell's voice. Splashing and screams grew louder as she stood there.

Can't save you now.

Darrell's cries intensified, then stopped. Silence surrounded her. Birds stopped chirping, and the only sound now was a strange tapping moving toward her through the trees. She searched for the source of the noise. Tapping, like fingers flicking a sheet of paper. Someone wavered behind a large tree before stepping out into the open. Darrell walked toward her, water dripping from his wet body, tapping onto the leaves covering the forest floor. He stopped several yards away, his face obscured in shadow.

"Emmie." His voice was a low growl.

Emmie kept silent and glanced toward Bobby. If she talked back, Bobby would hear her. Bobby would probably call the cops and it would piss John off before he arrested her for trespassing.

Darrell called her name again.

"I can't help you, kid," Emmie whispered and waved him away.

He gestured for her to follow him.

"I'm busy."

Darrell walked out of sight toward the lake. A minute later water splashed again, and the boy cried out louder, calling Emmie's name.

"All right, fine." Emmie took a deep breath and followed him, sneaking through the brush toward the lake. She would listen to him, if only to calm him so she could get back to snooping on Bobby.

Coming out into the open again, she stood on a narrow shoreline, in the same area where she had led police to Frankie's body when she was just seven years old.

The stench of dead fish hung in the air. Not far away, children laughed and splashed in the water near the beach.

Darrell struggled in the water a few yards out. He flailed his arms as he'd done so many times before as his head bobbed just above the surface. His white face and eyes locked onto her as he stretched out his hands.

"I can't rescue you," Emmie said.

He stretched out his hand further.

She opened her mouth to tell him that he was dead, even though that had never worked before. They either didn't listen or didn't believe her. Too absorbed in their own misery to listen to anyone.

Darrell sank below the surface. No bubbles after he submerged.

"You drown," she said. "I can't save you."

He reemerged a few seconds later and cried out for help again, gesturing for her to get closer. His face contorted in fear and emotional pain.

"It won't do any good, but fine..." She searched the area on the ground behind her and found a long branch.

As he choked and gasped for breath, she extended the branch toward him over the water. He seemed not to notice it.

"Grab it and I'll pull you in," she said. "Promise."

The branch hovered inches from his hands, but he acted as if he couldn't reach it.

"Help me help you." She moved it out as far as she could.

Darrell splashed and struggled with his hands inches away from the branch.

"Fine." Emmie kicked off her shoes and slipped off her socks, then stepped into the water up to her ankles so the branch would reach him.

The cool water soothed her feet, but the muck on the bottom of the lake nauseated her.

Darrell grabbed the branch and yanked it toward him.

Emmie held on but lost her balance. She tumbled forward, crashing into the water face down.

The water rushed in around her, cutting off her sight, hearing, and breath all at once. She let go of the branch, but Darrell grabbed her wrists and pulled her into a deeper section of the lake. She tried to stand, sliding her bare feet against the squishy, slick floor of the lake, but she couldn't find the bottom.

For a moment, she broke free and pushed to the surface. She heaved in a breath and screamed.

Darrell grabbed her wrists and pulled her under again, this time dragging her deeper down into the weeds and mud along the floor of the lake. The water gurgled as she descended.

She held her breath as her hands scraped across the lake bottom. Darrell's grip forced her fingers into the mud. She would drown if she didn't get out of there. What was Darrell planning to do to her? Bury her in the same spot where she'd found Frankie? Her fingers knocked against several small objects within the mud. Round objects. Marbles.

Is this what you want me to see?

She grabbed them and Darrell released his grip.

Someone else grabbed the back of her neck. A muscular hand.

❄ 25 ❄

Someone yanked Emmie up by her neck as she strained to hold her breath. She struggled to move away from Darrell while refusing to let the savior from above take her. Nothing was clear in the lake's murky water.

Yet she was pulled up, surging out of the water, gasping for air as the afternoon sun touched her face. Through the muffled water in her ears, a man's voice came through, "I got you. I got you."

Who's got me?

As the water drained from her eyes, the man's form came into view. She gagged on the putrid lake water and gasped for another breath.

"You'll be fine," the man said. "Hang on."

Her eyes adjusted to the light again. The water drained away from her face, and she was still buoyed by his firm grip around her neck as he threw another hand under her shoulder. She floated on the surface as she struggled to stay above the water.

"Easy there. Don't drown us both."

A shirtless man with a white beard stood beside her. A thinner version of Santa Claus. Bobby. Her heart raced.

She pulled away from his grasp, kicking and thrashing her

arms. Slipping away, she dropped a few inches, but now her feet touched the floor of the lake and she launched herself up again.

He pulled her closer toward the shore.

"No." She coughed. "Leave me alone."

"Leave you alone to drown? Not if I can help it. Just rest for a minute and catch your breath. I got you."

She would have run, except the struggle exhausted her. Her muscles burned, and she gasped for air—it took all her effort just to stay above the surface.

He helped her out of the water and sat her down on a patch of grass a few feet away from the shore. His shorts and shoes were dripping wet. Water drained over his face. "Just sit here for a minute. I'll be right back." Bobby lumbered off toward his house.

Emmie watched him leave. He was top-heavy—a large upper body with thin, sturdy legs. The result of building swimming strength over the years.

Darrell was gone, and the calm water reflected the cloudy sky. Her hand ached as she clutched the marbles. She opened her palm and looked at them. The same type of marbles she'd found at Frankie's gravesite. Could Frankie have been carrying them when he drowned? But who had put the other ones at his gravesite?

She coughed again and drew in another deep breath. No strength to get up, but every ounce of common sense told her to leave—run. She struggled to stand, her body wobbling as if she were drunk. Her chest and arms hurt, and she coughed. Her socks and shoes sat on the ground nearby. She crawled over and slipped on her socks over her wet, muddy feet. The outline of her cellphone jutting from her pocket caught her eye. She had taken it down in the water with her. Oh shit.

As she maneuvered to stand, Bobby broke through the trees nearby carrying a blanket.

"You just take it easy. That must've been a scary ordeal. Better to swim over near the beach. This section isn't safe." He wrapped the blanket over her shoulders and gestured for her to stay seated.

"I'll be all right," she said.

Bobby laughed and squatted next to her. "Sure, you will. Just tell me what you were thinking when you swam out there?" He looked at her clutched hand. "You aiming to retrieve something?"

She opened her palm and revealed the marbles.

He leaned back a few inches and gazed at her face. His eyes narrowed. "Oh, hell, is this about Franklin again?"

Her body stiffened, but she could still run away, if only she could catch her breath.

He shook his head. "He knew how to swim. I told the kids never to be out here on their own. The lake can be safer than a pool—no hard edges for them to hit, plenty of shallow water. I never did the deep training here, and I can't believe that Frankie, who was a good kid, not given to stunts at all, would come out here alone."

"It wasn't an accident."

Bobby furrowed his brows and eyed her. "You're the girl who found him, aren't you? I knew you looked familiar, but I wasn't sure. Look, I didn't kill the poor kid! Why would I? I wasn't even here—but I've felt like shit all these years that he could drown in my backyard, so close to the beach. What makes you think it wasn't an accident?"

"He told me."

His eyes widened and he leaned back as his head tilted to the side. "You had a vision about him?"

"He said *Bobby*."

Bobby stiffened and shook his head. "So you figured it was me? I don't have a motive for doing something so horrendous. If he said *Bobby*, then look for a Bobby with a motive, like someone who was sweet on his mother, maybe."

Emmie's gaze dropped to the blanket wrapped across her chest. She shivered at the implication. Only one person was ever sweet on Mary, as far as she knew. "All that happened afterwards."

"Well, that's the thing about small towns. You come swimming naked in the moonlight thinking nobody's watching, but I got ears, and I'm not so far away that I can't hear what's going on down here after sunset. We're all human, right?"

"You saw Mary and Robert down here?"

"Didn't see them, but plain as day, I knew what they were doing. That was before Frankie drowned. I'm not saying their rendezvous had anything to do with his death, but you're on the wrong path if you're thinking I had something to do with it." Bobby stared out over the water. "You need to follow your vision, your gift, and if it's like what you're saying, that it wasn't an accident, then think about why somebody would want to do something like that."

Emmie looked at the marbles. Darrell had wanted her to find them, but why? She turned them over in her fingers.

Bobby sighed. "Too many things lost in this lake over the years. You feeling better?"

Emmie nodded.

"You here alone?"

She hesitated to answer. "Yes."

"I suggest you get home and jump into the shower. The lake water's not clean like a pool is." Bobby stood up and turned away. "Keep the blanket."

❧ 26 ❧

E mmie's cellphone read 8:30 a.m.
Damn, girl, you slept a long time.
Takes a long time to recover from a traumatic day like yesterday.
She cleared her mind, but one word stuck with her. Bobby.

If not Bobby Norris, then only one possibility remained. Mary's husband, Robert, had never been suspected and she'd never heard anyone call him Bobby.

Maybe Frankie's name for him?

Norris's story of Mary and Robert skinny-dipping in the lake was difficult to believe. Mary wasn't the type to run off for a late-night rendezvous, and she couldn't imagine deadpan Robert romping in the lake naked like a teenager out past curfew. Norris could easily have mistaken them for another pair of lovebirds.

Was someone else involved in the case? Someone she'd forgotten or hadn't considered before?

Bobby.

Frankie, couldn't you have been a little more descriptive?

Norris's words came back to her. "Look for a Bobby with a motive."

Yeah, but now I got a Robert—and no motive.

She pushed the thoughts aside, mindlessly stepping through

her morning routine, before trudging downstairs to make herself a bowl of cold cereal. She sat on the couch in front of the television. The only channel worth watching was an old black-and-white comedy, one that reminded her of some TV shows her dad used to watch on Saturday mornings.

Her laptop sat open on her desk, but she left it powered off. Not much good having any electronics without Internet. Just one more day before the cable installation appointment. *Not soon enough.*

She checked the time on her cellphone. Finn would be there at ten o'clock. Sarah should be arriving soon too.

At nine thirty she went outside and sat on the front steps waiting for them. Just an empty lot across the street. A middle-aged couple without children had lived there in a small house for all the years she'd grown up, but now it was gone. They'd moved away and taken the house with them, ripping the whole thing right off its foundation, transplanting it to a different location across town. She'd never thought something like that was possible until she'd watched them do it, hauling it away in a single piece on a massive trailer.

What would a ghost do in that case? Would it leave with the house or stay with the land?

A wall of pine trees divided the empty lot from the next row of houses along the parallel street one block closer to town. Just open fields and trees to her left and behind the house, and one neighbor up the road to the right. As isolated as she could get, while still calling it city living.

A car turned onto her street. Sarah? Finn? No. A police car.

John, making a morning visit before work?

Any other time, the sight of his squad car would lighten her heart, but not now. Had Bobby reported her for trespassing? Emmie's heart sank and beat faster. *Shouldn't have gone out there, Em.*

It was John, all right. If she was in trouble with the law, he would try to help her any way he could, but he was no pushover.

He would arrest her, if that's what the law required, and it would be awkward as hell.

John stopped his car in her driveway. She waved as he got out and made his way up the sidewalk carrying a yellow manila folder.

Emmie stood and put on her bravest face. *If he arrests me, I won't argue.* "Hi John, is everything okay?"

He nodded once. "I was worried you might still be in bed. I wanted to talk with you about something."

Emmie's pulse thumped in her ears. She prepared her speech —*I'm so sorry, John. I had to go out to Bobby's place. I had no choice.* "Sure, what about?"

He eyed her as he opened the folder. "Enjoying some fresh air, I see."

She nervously chuckled. "I'm waiting for Sarah."

"Oh? Glad to hear you're making some connections again. Listen, the reason I stopped by was to talk to you about Franklin's case. After you came over to my office and had me pull out his file, I got to thinking, just like you wanted me to. Something didn't add up." John glanced at the top page in the stack of documents. "I found something unusual, but it could also be nothing. This has to do with the fact that, precisely, they don't set up most police departments like a CSI. We don't have the money to run fancy tests, the labs in the next big cities are usually overworked with pretty awful murders, and in the absence of huge evidence, we accept what is the most likely scenario. Franklin was taking swimming lessons at the lake, so it made sense that he drowned there. One little piece that didn't quite fit into the perfect box the investigators put the case into. I'm not saying it's anything, but..."

John flipped through the documents and stopped on one page that had the outline of a figure with arrows and scribbled notes scattered across the figure and margins. Emmie leaned in to see the notes, and John angled the papers toward her.

"But here's something puzzling—they found some bruises on

Frankie's thorax, between his neck and abdomen. They attributed it to branches hitting him in the water as his body drifted. Or maybe those bruises were from him struggling to stay above the water. Lots of other cuts and scrapes across his body as well."

Emmie's heart ached. "Branches didn't do that."

John paused but didn't nod. "I kept reading and found something else." He went to the page in question and tapped it. "The water in Frankie's lungs had no debris of the sort that would be found if he had drowned in the lake. I called the original investigator and asked him to explain the process they went through to determine the source of the bruises and of the water found in Franklin's lungs. He said what I just said—they hadn't bothered to investigate beyond simple tests because the cause of death was obvious in his case. You see, there was no suspicion of foul play when Bobby was cleared and Mary said Frankie was so eager to practice swimming all the time."

"Frankie wouldn't have gone down there alone," she repeated. "I knew him, John."

"Maybe, or maybe not. Kids *do* make irrational decisions. He might have felt the lake was a safe place to go, so it's not such a stretch to think he walked down there by himself."

Emmie calmed and grinned warmly. "I know you're trying to help me, John, but I don't just have an opinion about Frankie's death, I *know*. Someone murdered him."

"I wish I could understand how you know."

"Me too."

Someone's car revved in the distance. She glanced down the street, but no sign of Sarah or Finn. *Don't show up now, Finn—John has no patience for ghost hunters.*

John followed her gaze, then closed the folder. "I don't know what it means, yet. But I just wanted to share that with you before I head off to work. I felt it couldn't wait because of what we talked about yesterday."

Emmie nodded. "I appreciate your help. Every day, I think about Frankie."

"I haven't forgotten, either. Take care."

They hugged and John left. Only a minute after John's squad disappeared around the corner, Finn's silver Ford Fusion turned onto her street.

27

D *amn, Sarah, where are you? You're late.*
Emmie stood when Finn's car pulled into the driveway
and slipped her cellphone into her pocket.

He parked his car behind hers and briefly waved as he
climbed out and opened the back door on the driver's side.

"I'll grab some of my stuff." He lifted out a large silver
suitcase.

Emmie stepped forward. "You need help with that?"

"I got it, but it'll take a few trips." He lugged the silver case
up the sidewalk and shook her hand. "I can't wait to see what
you got for me."

Emmie paused, thinking about the basement and all that had
happened there. "Be careful what you wish for."

Finn grinned. "Lead the way."

She led him into the house. He paused in the living room,
eyeing the walls and ceiling as if he could sense the spirit world.
"So, this is the infamous Hanging House."

"This is it. I think we should go to the basement first. That's
where I captured the video yesterday. I've never done anything
like that before, and I'm sure my phone wasn't really the best
way to record it, but that's all I had."

Finn tapped the side of the suitcase. "My equipment will pick up just about any visual anomaly or magnetic disturbance, if it's here."

"It's definitely here."

He smiled politely. "Sure." He set down the suitcase in the middle of the living room and glanced around. "At least there's not much furniture to get in the way."

Emmie gave a small laugh and stepped sideways to block his view of the pile of belongings she'd left sitting in the middle of the floor. "I just moved back in after living in California for the last eight years. I took off right after high school ended."

"Because of the..."

"Spirits, yes. Among other things."

He threw her a look, as if deciding whether or not to enquire further, and paced around the perimeter of the room, inspecting the corners and darker areas. "I've heard a lot about this place. It's going to be interesting."

Interesting... that's a word for it. "I know the video I sent was low quality, but maybe you could see something in it."

"Lots of shadows, for sure, but you're right—not a great recording. Don't worry about that, though. If there's any paranormal activity in this house, I'll find it."

She scoffed. "It finds me every day. But what I see is a lot different from what's on the video."

"I'm sure it is. The trick is bridging the gap between us. I need to move beyond the regular optical images of a cellphone and use more sophisticated ways to gather real scientific data."

"Were you able to see Frankie's form in that video I sent?" Emmie took out her cellphone and scrubbed through the video until Frankie's torso and face stood out, at least to her. She showed the screen to Finn. "That's him there." Emmie pointed out his form.

Finn pursed his lips. "It's difficult to come to any conclusions with videos like that."

"It's him. I'm sure of it."

He nodded once. "I don't want to downplay your experience, but I intend to use scientific methods to verify it. Those shadows and lights could be something bouncing off the lens or light coming in through the window."

Emmie returned his nod. "Have you ever seen a spirit using your equipment?"

Finn paused. "It's difficult to say."

"So nothing you'd consider proof then?"

"Not really."

"What would satisfy you? If a spirit stood right here between us now, would that convince you?"

"Maybe."

Emmie scoffed and tensed. "So *seeing* one standing in front of you might not even change your mind?"

"People hallucinate sometimes. Ideally, I'd want evidence that I could scrutinize and verify through reproducible study."

Was it worth all the trouble with Finn? He must have sensed her irritation because he stepped forward, his face full of concern.

"I'm sorry," he said softly. "I wasn't suggesting you're hallucinating. For me, it's complicated. My damn brain gets in the way sometimes."

She calmed, having heard it all before from other skeptical people. No sense in trying to convince someone who didn't believe what she was saying. They had to experience it for themselves. "I get it." Emmie walked through the kitchen. "The basement is through here."

Following her closely, Finn carried the silver suitcase as she led him down into the basement. Their footsteps echoed, and the air cooled as they descended. *How would Bug Eyes react to another intruder in her house?*

"Can you tell me more about what happened yesterday?" Finn asked.

"Sure." Emmie spotted her pack of tarot cards on the floor

and picked them up. "I used these to communicate with the Hanging Girl and Frankie."

"Why tarot cards?"

"It helps me to focus."

Emmie continued, describing the face on the ceiling of her bedroom.

Finn listened without a reaction, then said, "That's a lot of activity in a short period of time."

"That's what my childhood was like in this house."

Finn stared up at the exposed pipes and wiring between the joists in the ceiling. "You didn't see ghosts when you lived in California?"

Emmie followed his gaze. Was he expecting to find clues to prove she was a fraud? *It's a crappy old house, Finn, but you just wait.* "I did if I wanted to, but I didn't want to. They faded into the background, unless one of them demanded my attention. Sometimes a kid would hound me to listen to them, sometimes relentlessly. Sometimes I could hear them, and sometimes not. I just avoided it as much as possible. No way I could help them, anyway."

"Yesterday's experience with Frankie and the Hanging Girl must have been shocking for you." He sounded sympathetic, but he was still following some electrical wiring to the back of the basement. Emmie trailed him.

"Yes. Just like old times. But the biggest thing about meeting Frankie again was the one word he said to me. Well, he didn't really *say* it, he mouthed it, because I couldn't hear him. Bobby."

"Bobby?"

"Yeah, I know it's weird, but remember that suspect named Bobby Norris from the library article? He was Frankie's swimming coach."

Finn stopped and met her eyes. "Could he have killed a boy? Is that what you mean?"

Emmie shrugged. "I met Norris yesterday, and I'm not so sure. Frankie was trying to tell me something, but I couldn't hear him well. I have to figure out a way to communicate with him again without all the interference from the other spirits. When I open myself up to communicating with the other world, there's no way to control who gets to talk and who doesn't. Everybody talks at once. It's overwhelming."

Finn continued scanning the ceiling and walls. He walked over to the far wall and unceremoniously opened a door into a small room beneath Mary's apartment. Emmie didn't stop him. She had to remember she wanted him there and not resent the fact that he was treating the place as if it weren't *her* house. She shouldn't be like Bug Eyes. He flipped on the light. "What's in here?"

The windowless room was bare now. Only a stack of wooden shelves remained, which her dad had used to display occult memorabilia. If Finn hadn't opened the door, she might never have peeked in. "My dad used to study the occult in there. I'm sure he loved it because it's a dark room, no sunlight to spoil the fun, and far away from everybody else. He would go in and study and chant with the door closed."

"So you've been more or less raised on the knowledge of the occult."

"Yes, but we weren't witches or devil worshipers or any of that stuff."

He raised an eyebrow. "Ouija boards or pentagrams or candles, any of that?"

"All of those. Just without the black robes and goat sacrifices." Emmie smirked.

Finn closed the door, and they made their way back over to his equipment until they stood on opposite sides. "How many spirits were there yesterday in your recording?"

"At first just a couple, but then others arrived, and I'm sure if I had left the channel open it would have been dozens within an hour. The channel acts like a magnet. It's unbelievably upsetting to witness." Her pulse thumped faster in her ears just thinking about it.

"Then the Hanging Girl was getting in the way of talking with Frankie?"

Emmie nodded, thinking of the hatred in her eyes.

Finn had opened the metal suitcase and removed a camera, along with a tripod and a bundle of cables.

You'll sound crazy, Em.

She folded her arms and watched him untangle a black cord. For a moment, she regretted letting him inside the house. Maybe it would have been better to keep it all buried away in her mind and never discuss it again with anyone. That plan had *mostly* worked during her years in California.

He doesn't believe you.

What does it matter? No more running from the truth.

Finn paused and gazed at her as if he'd read her mind, "You're very brave to deal with this so well. Is the Hanging Girl like a poltergeist? Throwing things, slamming doors, terrorizing you?"

"Sort of like that. When I was a little girl, she only scared me. I could talk all night about the encounters I've had with her."

"Did you tell your mom and dad about it?"

"Yes, many times. They believed me, but they didn't do anything to stop it. Actually, I'm sure they bought this house for the sole reason it was haunted."

Finn connected a video camera to a tripod and adjusted some settings on the digital display after turning it on. His actions were methodical and precise, as if the data he'd collect was monumentally important to him. "What was their interest in haunted houses?"

"I'm not sure where it started for them. I never asked."

He stopped and gazed at her, as if he were seeing her for the first time. *Pity in his eyes, as if he was looking at an abused child. I don't want pity.* She glanced away.

Finn looked around the room once more. "Can you tell me where the circuit breaker is located?"

He still thinks I might be a fraud?

"Sure. Over there." Emmie pointed and led him to the laundry room.

"I need to find any potential magnetic or electrical interference. Just ruling out the most common causes for anomalies." He flipped open the circuit breaker and inspected the wiring. "This is very outdated wiring—potentially dangerous. I'm not an electrician, but you should get this updated as soon as possible."

That and everything else in the house. "You're probably right."

Again, he was looking at her a little more thoughtfully, and his eyes dropped to his shoes as he said, "Look, don't take anything personally. I know most people will think you're either scary or crazy. I swear I don't. I want to help figure this out, okay? You're telling me stuff that has terrified you your whole life, and it can't be easy to talk about it."

She waved a hand. "And I don't want to make my parents sound evil. Maybe I did, a moment ago. The truth is that as far back as I can remember, I've seen spirits. One of my first memories is of being at a picnic and pointing out a skinny blonde schoolgirl who was playing with a young boy at the swing set. I laughed at the way she was dressed, one of those school uniforms from long ago, and I told my parents how funny she looked. My parents didn't see her at all, but they believed me. I guess most parents would tell their kids they were hallucinating, but my parents encouraged me. Maybe that's why I developed this sense, because they kept pushing me to point out anything unusual."

He motioned toward his equipment as they moved back. "And I can't judge your parents, exactly. I know I can get pretty obsessive, trying to find proof of ghosts. I guess they just did the same another way. It's too bad that it involved their child, is all."

"There's something else. You want to see ghosts," she said firmly. "But you have to understand, the Hanging Girl's got a lot of rage, and it's not so fun to have that anger targeted at you. It's terrifying."

He swallowed. "I can imagine."

"I wonder if you can..." She stopped and took a deep breath, realizing how much he had made her talk with his impersonal, journalistic way of asking questions. Strangely, she did feel lighter, which allowed her to continue, "And the thing is, my parents used to say I should make peace with the ghosts, but that girl doesn't want peace. She wants me out of the house."

"What can she do about that?"

Emmie hesitated, remembering the last incident. "She grabbed me yesterday." Carefully, she pulled down the edge of her collar.

He stared from a distance at first, then circled around the camera equipment and touched her collar, examining her neck. "She *hurt* you?"

"I barely got away before she strangled me."

"So she can *touch* you?"

He was on the edge between fascination and disbelief; she could see him tottering there.

"That's just it. I didn't think she could; my mother kept telling me it was impossible. But the girl had the house all to herself for years, and then I came back." Emmie nodded a few times, looking squarely into Finn's eyes. "This is her house, she says. And now she is more powerful and angrier than ever."

❧ 28 ❧

"I'm going to summon her again," Emmie said, turning toward the exit, "when you're ready."

"You're planning to bring back the Hanging Girl today?" Finn sounded a bit doubtful now, and added, "Isn't that a terrifying thought after what you said happened yesterday?"

"Definitely, but I'm not planning to communicate with her. I'll focus on Frankie instead and bring him back. Maybe I can get him to tell me something more than just the one word this time. I know he's trying to tell me more. I'm glad that you can be here to record it with me this time."

Finn stared at the ceiling. "Would you mind if I looked around the rest of the house? I need to get my bearings."

She smiled. "In case you have to make a quick escape?" Emmie motioned toward the basement stairs. "Be my guest."

Finn smiled back, not without some irony. "I appreciate it."

They returned to the living room.

Emmie nodded at the open doorway separating the living room from Mary's old apartment. "That's where Frankie used to live."

Finn walked into Mary's apartment. He stopped and pointed at the number in the ceiling. "Was that always here?"

"Not until recently."

After studying it for a moment, he looked at the windows and door. "A prankster? Someone who vandalized your place?"

"I don't think so. A gift from either the Hanging Girl or Frankie, I'm not sure which one."

"What's the number six supposed to mean?"

"I thought it was an address, a house number, but I was wrong. I'm not sure now."

"Interesting."

This word again.

Finn stepped around the living room and glanced into the two bedrooms and the bathroom. "I'll make sure to spend some time recording data in this apartment as well. You never know what we might uncover. I brought some duplicate equipment with me to record in multiple rooms at the same time, but I'd have to move it from room to room as we go. Maybe starting up here would be better for now, since the number on the ceiling might be evidence of something happening. Then we can move down into the basement a little later. I'm guessing the basement is where the primary energy is focused?"

"Yes. We played down there a lot and we would play hide and seek as well as mess around with my parents' Ouija board."

"All right. I'll get the rest of my equipment now. It'll take some time to set up, but once it's in place, we're ready to go."

"Do you need some help?"

"Sure."

Finn and Emmie walked back out to his car, unloading two more stuffed black suitcases and two large tripods. Grabbing the larger one, Finn rolled it along the sidewalk on its wheels. "If anybody's watching us, they're probably thinking I'm moving in."

Emmie glanced up at the blackened upstairs windows. "She's watching us now."

He stopped short and followed her gaze. "The one who's mad that you're here thinks I'm moving in as well? Great. Can you see her?"

"No, but she's there. She's always there."

They took the equipment into Mary's old apartment. As Finn removed each piece and set it up, he explained what it did. "This one is an EMF device. It measures magnetic frequencies so that if there's a spirit in the room, I should be able to witness an aberration of the data in that area as long as there is no obvious magnetic disturbance nearby, then we could call that a possible hit."

She gave a small, wry laugh. "Listen to you. Could call it a possible maybe remotely..."

"Now, would I have all this stuff if I were easy to convince?" He lifted out a camcorder and held it up as if it were an exotic bit of scientific equipment. "You can only find this rare piece of equipment in all major department stores around the country, and pretty much everywhere online."

"Then it's a good thing I found the most professional of ghost hunters to help me."

"Exactly. But what makes this beauty different is that it's got night vision. These are the cameras that all the ghost TV shows love to use. They all have these things because it can see in the dark." Finn held up another device. "And then we have and MFN FM frequency screener that records the sounds of anything in the room, especially those at odd frequencies. The human ear can't pick up a lot of sounds, but this thing can."

He took yet another device. The house was beginning to look like a movie set.

"And this one is a motion detector, so if you had any kind of pets in the house, I would ask you to keep them out of the room. Even if you have rats in the walls and any of them crawl around the floor, the motion detector would trigger and start the night vision camera to record."

"I'd be very happy if it was just rats."

"You may get your wish. You'd be surprised at how many"— Finn made quote marks with his fingers—"*haunted houses* turn out to be nothing more than rodent infestations." At the next piece of equipment, he said, "And then you have the heat sensors that will detect if there's any cool spots in the area. The theory goes that ghosts produce pockets of cold air around them as they travel from room to room. Have you experienced anything like that here?"

Emmie nodded. "I know this is an old house—it's drafty, especially in the winter—but the spirits I've encountered have all had that trait."

Finn looked at the device. "I'll take that into consideration when we look at the data, but it seems to help." He pulled out some flashlights. "And then we have these. We use these when we need to run like hell." Finn laughed. "They've come in handy a few times, as you might expect."

"You mean, you *did* see a spirit?"

"Not as such," he said, closing one eye as he considered his answer. "Had a few frights, though. What I would consider *close calls*."

"I guess enough of a fright to make you keep looking?"

"What am I going to do with all this stuff if I don't keep looking?" He grinned. "I've got more at home too."

"Must be an expensive hobby."

"It is, but it's my only habit right now, so I can afford it. I don't drink or smoke. No drugs. *And* I'm single, so that helps."

Pulling out a set of large goggles, he put them on his head.

"For example, I'd much rather find ghosts than raccoons or the spotted owl with these. They are night-vision goggles. And I like to monitor everything while I'm recording to prevent any shenanigans that might occur. Some hosts *do* try to pull pranks on me. In your case, I'm not concerned about that, but I'll probably use them, anyway. No offense."

"No problem. You might end up taking them off if things go like yesterday."

"I'd love to see the real thing." He didn't seem spooked now, surrounded by all his gadgets. "Getting scientific evidence... I'd love to be the one to finally prove the existence of spirits to the world. Not just to prove all the cynics wrong, but rather to prove the existence of an expanded reality beyond our own."

"Today might be your lucky day."

Finn smiled. "Then I should make sure that everything is charged up and ready to go." He untangled some cables and plugged in the cameras to the walls. "I need to spend some time calibrating everything, but it's difficult to do that in daylight. Some of it will have to wait until it gets dark."

"Do what you need to do." Emmie leaned against the wall, watching him. "I'll just wait here."

Undisturbed by her presence, Finn laid out the equipment on the floor and organized the different elements. His process fascinated her. He was so meticulous and calculated in his movements. He'd no doubt gone through the steps many times before, exploring other haunted houses.

He lifted a DSLR camera and aimed the lens at her. "Do you mind?"

She broke away from gazing at his fingers working the controls. "Oh, sorry, yes. I mean, no, that's okay." She stood a little straighter before he snapped a photo and checked it on the camera's screen.

"Sometimes just a simple photo reveals unusual things."

"Anything?"

He shook his head and set the camera down next to a tripod. "I still need to study the data I collected near Franklin's grave site."

"Don't bother." As he looked up at her, she shrugged. "Do you really think ghosts hang around there? Sometimes they show up at funerals, but mostly ghosts hang out where there's life. Where *they* lived. Sometimes where they died..."

"I guess that makes sense," he said slowly. "I never thought of it that way."

"That's one of the reasons I like to go to the graves. It's my oasis away from the spiritual world."

"All right." Finn glanced over Emmie's shoulder toward the

window that looked out into the backyard. "What about the Hanging Tree, then? That's where the girl died, right? Do you see her there?"

"Yes."

"Could we go there? Or is it scary for you?"

Without a word, she walked to the door and turned back, waiting for him. Finn put the camera strap around his neck and grabbed another device off the floor.

The door wailed open, almost as if complaining. First time she'd gone through that door in years. She waited for Finn to catch up before leading him across the grassy yard.

The garage stood on the right at the end of the driveway. One of these days she'd need to go through all the junk inside it. John and Mary had packed everything left over after the auction following her parents' death. *Plenty of surprises in there, I'm sure.*

Soon the Hanging Tree came into view behind the garage. The tree stretched toward the sky like a gnarly, decaying hand until they rounded the corner and it stood in full view before them. A thick lower branch jutted off to the side like an arm reaching toward the garage.

"When I first saw the Hanging Girl," Emmie said, "she was hanging from that main branch."

Finn snapped a few pictures and asked in an almost solemn tone, "Do you see her now?"

"No, thank God."

After a few more pictures from different angles, he hung the camera over his neck again and extended the other device toward the tree. He pivoted it slowly. "What's the process for invoking spirits to appear for you?"

"It's not that difficult, but it seems to help a lot if I have something to focus on. Otherwise, like I said, I'm just an open radio channel calling for all the spirits to come and talk. Last night I had a tarot card in my hand—one particular card, The Tower—because when I think of that card, I think of the Hanging Girl and the tree. She showed up all right, but Frankie showed up too, I guess because when I think of The Tower card, I also think of Frankie and the treehouse he had right there." She nodded at the branch. "Technically, it wasn't *his* treehouse. The previous owners of the house must have built it for their kid, but I never went in there because of the Hanging Girl. So Frankie adopted it as his own. I had no problem with that."

It took a moment for him to ask. "These kids...What do you think they want?"

"Help, I guess. Even the Hanging Girl probably needs help, but how can I help someone like that? Even now, as a grownup, I have no idea what to do about them. It's so tragic to see their faces. Imagine walking around with a bowl of plastic fruit and having starving children reaching out toward you, begging for food. They think the food is real, but there's no way you can feed them."

"Well..." he said softly. "No wonder you don't want to think about it."

"Most of them have open wounds or major trauma to their bodies." Emmie's eyes teared up. "And the worst part is, I can only see children. All these kids begging for help, and I'm powerless."

She shook her head to clear it and walked up to the tree. Were they there, either of them? Finn walked beside her. Anxiety fluttered in her chest, but the jarring chill of a spirit's presence was gone.

He approached the tree from different angles and took readings on the branch that had supported Frankie's treehouse long ago.

"Anything?" Emmie asked.

"Nothing yet." He stepped back. "But I guess I'm done here for now."

Emmie turned back toward the house without waiting to hear anymore. She was relieved they hadn't seen anything— happy for the respite from all the drama.

The glass in the back door and the side windows reflected

the trees and sky as she approached. The breeze stirred her hair and a bird chirped in an overhead branch.

A scream caught her off guard and she shuddered. The muffled cries from someone inside, then violent pounding on the door. She froze at the bottom step.

In the window next to the door, the reflections transformed into the face of a panicked woman.

❧ 29 ❧

Half an hour before, Sarah had parked her car along the edge of the street and walked up the sidewalk toward Emmie's front door, clutching two cups of coffee she'd purchased from Mary's cafe on the way to liven up Emmie's morning.

Someone had parked an unfamiliar car behind Emmie's. That ghost-hunter guy Emmie had mentioned. She peeked in the driver's side window as she passed it. Clean. A laptop and a clipboard sitting on the passenger seat.

Balancing the coffee when she reached the door, she pressed the doorbell with her elbow.

No response after thirty seconds.

She pressed it again and peered in through the small windows beside the front door. The door leading into the back apartment was wide open. Emmie had to be there somewhere.

She rang the doorbell one more time, still staring into the house. No movement or sounds or any sign of her. Where could she be?

Maneuvering the cups into one hand, she knocked and rang the doorbell again.

Still no answer.

Must be downstairs, or up in her room. The coffee's aroma stirred

Sarah's thirst. She'd promised herself she'd wait to drink it with Emmie, but the smell... She took a small sip. Then another.

I can go in. She won't mind. She knows I'm coming.

Sarah cracked open the door and poked her head in.

"Emmie?" she called out.

No reply, but someone was talking in the distance. A girl's voice. Was it coming from upstairs or the basement? A little from both. *Must be Emmie.*

She reached back and rang the doorbell a third time, just to be polite, before stepping inside and closing the door behind her.

"Emmie? Are you there? I'm coming inside. Ready or not."

Sarah moved in past the entryway and glanced around. No sign of Emmie. She walked into the kitchen and set the coffee on the counter. She picked her cup back up and took another small sip. *I can't be expected to resist this temptation. I'm only human.*

Walking over to the refrigerator, she peeked inside. Diet cola, a bag of limes, a few bottled waters, leftover fast food, and various condiments. No sign of home-cooked anything.

She doesn't know how to cook. I can teach her.

Something thumped below her feet. Something from below the floorboards, a groaning, and then more knocks as the sound moved across the floor toward the basement door.

What the heck is going on? Is she working down there?

The basement door stood wide open. Noises echoed downstairs. A female voice.

"Emmie?" she called.

It had to be her, though it sounded a little high-pitched.

Sarah walked through the doorway and looked at the bottom of the stairs. "Emmie?"

All the lights were on. The voice grew louder as Sarah took one step down.

"Emmie? Anybody there? It's me, Sarah. I brought some food."

They had to be working in the basement, but how could they

not hear her? She didn't want to interrupt their work or scare anyone. She hesitated and called out again. She clomped down the stairs a little more loudly than normal to let them know she was there. A girl broke out laughing somewhere in the basement, as if she'd gotten the punchline to a great joke.

"Okay, Em, I'm coming down. Are you playing with me?"

She reached the bottom of the stairs and turned the corner. Electronics were sprawled out over the basement floor. Cameras, wires, tripods. Maybe Emmie was recording something with the ghost hunter. The stale air reminded Sarah of the encounter they'd had with the Hanging Girl the day before.

"I'm not sure if you're down here or not, but I thought I'd stop by and see how you're doing."

Sarah stopped at the bottom of the stairs and listened for the girl's voice again. Something wasn't right. A chill passed through her. If Emmie was down there, no need to bother her. Better to wait upstairs, anyway.

No, get the heck out of there.

The girl murmured from across the room. No sign of her. Another laugh erupted.

Not Emmie's voice. Her pulse pounded in her ears.

Before she could turn back to the stairway, an empty tripod rattled, then flew across the room at her. She jumped out of the way as the top end of the tripod smashed into the wall behind her like a giant lawn dart. One of the legs brushed her arm as it flew by.

She shrieked then charged up the stairs, her footsteps thundering under her until she got halfway and the door leading back into the kitchen slammed shut.

Bad, very bad.

The lights went out.

"Emmie!" She climbed faster. A window in the door ahead, leading to the side of the house, provided enough light, but she flipped the switch along the way a few times without luck. She pulled on the door to the kitchen.

Locked, yet it gave a little as if someone were holding it on the other side. She yanked and turned the handle, but it wouldn't open. The side door also wouldn't budge.

Her heart raced as she stared back down into the darkness. Nothing moving within the shadows, but she only stared for a moment. Something knocked against the sides of the walls and the steps. The glint of metal moved up out of the darkness. A tripod appeared, rattling and knocking against the walls and stairs as it moved like a feeble three-legged dog toward her.

The air chilled and her legs weakened as she pounded on the door with her fists and screamed. "Emmie! I'm trapped, Emmie!"

The tripod clattered across the ceiling toward her with its legs spread out, facing down. Hovering above her, it stopped. Its legs curled into loops as if it were melting and twisted around until they formed three nooses.

A girl's laughter rose from the darkness at the bottom of the stairs. "One for each of you."

Sarah gasped and struggled with the door again. She pounded it with her fists, then grabbed the door handle with both hands and heaved herself back with all her strength.

The door whipped open, throwing Sarah against the opposite wall where she toppled to the floor and nearly tumbled over the edge of the stairway. The girl's laughter grew louder. Sarah recovered and stood as the tripod fell and crashed down the stairway. She rushed into the kitchen a moment before the door slammed shut behind her.

Trembling and aching from hitting the wall, she hurried through the kitchen toward the front door.

Just get outside. She grabbed the door's handle and pulled.

It wouldn't open.

"No! Emmie!"

She pounded her fists and spun around as panic welled up. The door to Mary's apartment was wide open. *Another way out.* She charged across the house to the back door.

The girl's laughter followed her.

30

Emmie froze for a moment, staring at the face. Not the Hanging Girl this time, but Sarah. Her eyes were wide, and the cries she mouthed were muffled as she slapped her palm on the glass.

Leaping up the steps, Emmie rushed toward her and opened the door. Sarah collapsed into her arms, nearly stumbling down the stairs as she struggled to get away.

"Sarah, what's going on?" Emmie tried to raise her face and look into her eyes.

"I couldn't get out." Sarah stared back at the house and heaved in a deep breath.

"The doors were locked?"

"I don't know. I couldn't open anything."

Emmie glanced back at the Hanging Tree. "It's her. She's grown stronger since I've come back."

"I'm just glad to be out of there." Sarah folded her arms over her chest as if comforting herself.

Finn rushed up the steps. "Did you see anyone?"

Her eyes focusing on Finn as if she had only then remembered he was coming over, Sarah half shrugged, half shook her head. "I went to the basement because I heard a girl's voice. I thought it was you, Em. Then... I know this sounds weird... one of those camera tripods flew across the room and almost hit me. Well, it *did* hit me after I ran to the top of the stairs. I didn't see anyone, but I know someone was there."

"Are you okay?" Emmie checked Sarah.

Sarah nodded. A confused look spread over her face. "Is that what you went through growing up in this house, Em?"

"Not quite as bad as this." Emmie turned to Finn. "But it'll only get worse. I need to confront her now."

"Maybe you shouldn't go back in there." Sarah gripped Emmie's hand.

"I have to, or she'll just keep terrorizing us. I can't even talk to Frankie with her in the way."

Sarah noticed the digital audio recorder in Finn's hand. "I hope you brought something to get rid of her."

Finn shook his head regretfully. "I'm not sure I'd know how to do that."

"Grab a shield before going back in there."

"It was that bad?" he asked.

"For me it was."

Emmie comforted Sarah. "I'm sorry I didn't hear you at the door. I took him out back to look at the tree."

"It's okay." Sarah attempted a smile. "I brought you a coffee."

"Thank you." She hugged Sarah. "Sorry about what happened in there."

"It's not your fault."

"Do you want to see a doctor? Or need a ride home? I wouldn't blame you for leaving now."

"You're going to do that thing again in the basement?" Sarah glanced over her shoulder at the back door. "What we did yesterday?"

"Yes."

Sarah cringed. "It's not safe down there."

"That's why I have to stop her before this gets worse."

Although her face was pale, Sarah nodded. "I'll stay."

Emmie led them into the house, crossing through Mary's old apartment and around to the kitchen. She spotted the coffee on the counter but didn't stop. All the time, Finn held out his digital recorder as if he might capture some elusive haunted whisper. He was grinning.

"You're enjoying this, aren't you?" Emmie's face warmed.

"I'm cautiously optimistic."

"Spirits aren't like fish you catch and then mount on your wall. They're people with seriously screwed-up issues. Some of them, like the Hanging Girl, would love to see all of us dead."

Finn lowered his audio recorder. "I didn't mean any disrespect."

"It's not a game."

A girl's laughter came from the basement.

"Did you hear that?" Sarah asked.

"Yes," Emmie said.

"Hear what?" Finn asked.

Sarah shivered. "That's her, isn't it?"

"Yes." Emmie smiled sympathetically. "This is why I didn't have a lot of friends growing up. Not a great place for sleepovers."

"It's the quality, not the quantity, right?" said Sarah.

"That's true." Emmie glanced over at the open door going down into the basement. "You want to wait for us up here? You've already been through a lot."

"No, I'd rather be with you."

"All right, let's go." Emmie pushed the door to the basement open further, but it knocked against a solid object. She peeked around the corner. A mangled tripod sat at the top of the stairs.

Sarah gestured toward it. "That's what hit me."

Finn leaned down and took it. "That's bizarre." He strained to unbend the metal legs that had curled around to form three loops. "You didn't see anybody?"

"No. I only heard the laughter, and she said she wants us to hang."

Emmie flipped the switch on and off twice. No light.

"Oh, I forgot to mention," Sarah said. "The power's out."

Emmie sighed. "Yeah, that happens." She hurried back into the kitchen and grabbed the flashlight from the counter. Another trip to the breaker box.

They went down into the darkness after her, stopping at the bottom of the stairs to scan the surroundings. All the equipment was still where they'd left it, minus one tripod, and no sign of the Hanging Girl. Emmie turned right into the laundry room and opened the circuit panel. Same switch every time. Third one down on the left. She reset it and the lights burst on.

"She likes to do that a lot." Emmie turned off the flashlight. "Expect it to happen again."

Finn went ahead on his own around the corner. "I'll finish getting set up."

Sarah leaned into her. "I'm sorry I ever doubted you. I never imagined I would experience something like that."

"At least she didn't hurt you. It never used to be this bad growing up. Something definitely changed after I moved back in."

"I can't even imagine how a kid could have put up with that fear every night."

Emmie looked at the floor. "I'm not a kid anymore. Now I need to do something about the bully making my life miserable —get her out of the way, so I can finally talk to Frankie."

❧ 31 ❧

E mmie sat on a folding chair in the center of the basement. Ghost hunter surveillance equipment surrounded the room Finn had deemed the best place for *perhaps* capturing data during the visit. She removed the first tarot card from the deck, The Tower.

"Are you ready?" Finn asked.

"Not really, but I'll give it my best shot." Emmie took a deep breath and narrowed her eyes. She held up the tarot card with both hands.

Frankie's treehouse stood out in her mind. A chill passed through her, something greater than just the cool basement air. The Hanging Girl was close by, and it wouldn't take long before the confrontation started. Emmie tensed as the wall between her and the spirit world melted away.

Finn and Sarah stood several feet behind the video camera in front of her.

Emmie's mind cleared. The treehouse and The Tower card image appeared like white lines on a black background. Floating, shifting veins of electricity flooded her eyesight before the voices grew louder.

Then the chatter began. It was like someone walking out of a silent, sealed room toward a crowded street. The further she dropped into her meditative focus, the louder the voices grew. And they came from everywhere. All around her. They circled in the air and streamed in, dozens of children crying out for help.

One voice rose above the others. Not a pleasant sound. Drawing closer, the Hanging Girl screamed. Emmie squirmed in her seat as pressure built in her mind. She had to block them, somehow, stop them from getting too close to her channel.

It's already too much.

The Hanging Girl's face flashed before her as she charged toward Emmie with her arms out, her fingers extended, as if to claw out her eyes. A noose hung around the girl's neck, the other end of the rope fading several feet behind her.

"You can't live in this house anymore," Emmie cried out, opening the channel further. The voices grew louder.

A scratchy voice replied, "You don't listen." The Hanging Girl's face hovered in front of Emmie, who winced at the scene around her. Dozens of ghastly children's faces.

"You will listen to me now." The Hanging Girl lurched forward and clutched Emmie's throat.

Emmie grabbed the girl's wrists and pulled, but her airway closed and she stopped breathing. Her neck muscles strained to twist away. She mouthed the first few words of the nursery rhyme from her youth. A gasping, "Now I lay... me down to..." The Hanging Girl loosened her grip but didn't back away.

"You can't escape from me anymore." The girl's wide grin stretched even further. "I have you."

"Tell me..." Emmie said between gasping for breath. "Tell me what you want."

"You know it's my house," the girl screamed. "I want you out."

"No, it's my house now. You're dead."

Somewhere upstairs, glass shattered. "My house!"

"Did someone murder you?"

The girl's expression changed. She shuddered and stepped

back, losing the searing hatred for a moment before the rope around her neck stretched tight up to the ceiling as if pulled higher by an unseen executioner. She glanced up at the rope, then down toward her feet. Her eyes widened as the rope yanked her upward, snapping her neck with a nauseating crack. Her eyes bulged and her tongue flopped out.

The Hanging Girl gagged, convulsing with burning red eyes until the rope around her neck faded too. She clutched at her neck as the familiar grin replaced the terror.

"My house." The girl reached for Emmie's neck again.

"Is that how you died?"

"Would you like to try it?"

Emmie shifted back in her seat as the Hanging Girl lurched forward and grabbed her hair, pulling her head back as if to slit her throat.

"I'll drag you out of here on a rope." The girl laughed.

"Now I lay me down to sleep, I pray the Lord my soul to keep."

The Hanging Girl calmed and loosened her grip on Emmie's hair.

Emmie took advantage of the moment's reprieve to search the crowd of child spirits. Frankie's form appeared far off in the background. A fuzzy silhouette, but it was him. "Frankie, can you hear me? I want to talk to Frankie."

Emmie focused on Frankie only. She pictured him in his tree-house. Other children approached from all sides, crying out to her. "You don't listen to us." "See me." "Help me, I'm lost." They clawed at Emmie's clothes and skin. So many lost souls. Their voices rose as they crowded in, each of them telling a story on top of the others. Nothing came through clearly except the horrible visions of the death each had suffered.

Emmie reached out to one boy with bloated white skin. His face swelled unnaturally, as if he would explode or pop. Some had committed suicide, despite their young ages. Some had been murdered, and some simply didn't realize they were dead, still holding on to their physical existence.

"I see you all. I'll help you somehow, but I don't know how." Emmie's eyes teared up as they grabbed at her, and she didn't resist. Their pain surged as they touched her. All their sadness poured into her and welled up inside. So much hopelessness and fear.

"Frankie!" Emmie cried.

Sarah's voice called out from somewhere in the fog, "Emmie, are you okay?"

She nodded, but she wasn't okay. Far from it.

"Frankie, are you there?" Emmie screamed.

Frankie's form coalesced behind the others and then moved forward, pushing through the crowd of faces that enveloped her vision in every direction.

His voice came through more clearly as he moved closer.

"Frankie!" Emmie called. "Come here."

"I'm right here," Frankie said. "Don't you see me?"

Then she did.

Frankie stepped up beside the Hanging Girl, his eyes wide with fear. Emmie reached toward him, but the Hanging Girl wedged herself between them.

Emmie stared into the girl's eyes. "Move out of the way."

"My house. My rules."

"I will talk with my friend." Emmie's voice wavered, although she meant it.

The Hanging Girl approached. The rope around her neck reappeared, and she clawed at it. "You will get me out of this."

"I will," Emmie said.

The girl let out a guttural groan, then backed away, allowing Frankie to move forward.

For the first time, Frankie stood before her completely as she remembered him.

"Emmie," Frankie gurgled. The sound grew clearer as he

inched closer. A grin erupted on his face. "Emmie, what card do I have in my pocket?"

The question caught her off guard. "Can we play later, Frankie? I want to help you. Who killed you?"

Frankie's grin grew wider. "I've been trying to tell you."

"I'm sorry, I didn't understand. Who is it?"

"I want to play first. What card do I have in my pocket?"

"Frankie, please don't play now. We don't have much time. I can't keep this up for very long."

Frankie patted his pocket to suggest the card inside. "Guess."

Emmie sighed. She focused on the card in his pocket. She saw it clearly. "I can see it, Frankie. It's The Lovers."

"You're right!" Frankie pulled the card out and held it up so she could see. Seeing the card in front of her, she realized her mistake. A big mistake.

Six—Frankie had drawn the number on the ceiling in Mary's apartment. The Lovers was card number six.

"But then you weren't pointing to Bobby Norris's house number?"

Frankie shook his head. "It's a card game, Emmie. Don't you remember?"

The Lovers. Her mind raced back to Mary and Robert standing side by side in all the photos on the walls of the cafe and at Mary's house. How long had they been lovers? Before Frankie's death? Swimming naked in the lake?

Robert in another photo, in Venice with his brother after his marriage broke up *and before he and Mary were supposed to be together.*

Frankie's marbles were Murano glass. From Venice.

The marbles! That is why Darrell had made her find them. Not to discover what she already knew, that Frankie had been in that water—but to make her understand that *Robert* had given him those marbles.

"Robert killed you?" she whispered in horror. "Did you know him then? Did you call him Bobby?"

Frankie shook his head and stared at the floor.

"Bobby Norris killed you?" Emmie insisted, confused.

Frankie scowled at her. "The card! You just guessed it right! How come you forgot already?"

"I'm sorry, Frankie, I..."

"I guess I will have to show you." Frankie held out his hand.

Emmie reached her hand toward him. Their palms touched on a higher level. The icy emptiness of Frankie's spirit chilled her skin. He tugged her hand with a force like a magnet, pulling her. His presence swarmed around her wrist and arm.

The Hanging Girl and surrounding spirits parted quietly as she stood, allowing Frankie to lead her toward the bathroom door at the bottom of the stairs below Mary's apartment.

The door creaked open on its own.

Sarah and Finn rustled behind Emmie, following her into the darkness of the bathroom. Finn had taken the camera from the tripod and held it now, still filming. Without switching on the light, Emmie peered into the bathtub where the vision of Frankie now transformed to him bathing as a child, with Mary on her knees next to the tub, her chest and arms hanging inside.

No, no, no...

He laughed, splashing in the water, until Mary jumped forward and pressed down on his legs and chest.

She swatted away his arms as he clawed at the sides of the tub, scrambling to sit up as his face submerged. He rose above the surface for a moment, calling out, "Mommy, Mommy, Mommy," before Mary pushed him back down again.

❧ 32 ❧

Frankie's vision faded as Emmie took a huge gulp of painful air.

A heavy bitterness swept through her like poison. The earlier communication had been so weak. The name hadn't come through clearly. She'd mixed up the words. Not Bobby...

Mommy.

So simple, yet so difficult to believe. The truth had stared her in the face.

"Oh, Mary. Why?" Emmie broke down and began sobbing.

Frankie faded off again behind the others. The Hanging Girl glared at her as all the spirits disappeared.

Emmie hadn't heard it right. The most awful possible cry: *Mommy, Mommy, Mommy.*

Sarah and Finn were beside Emmie. Sarah put her arm over Emmie's shoulders. "Are you okay, Em?"

Tears ran down Emmie's cheeks, brushing past the corner of her mouth. She turned to Sarah. "Did you see him?"

"No." Sarah glanced at the bathtub.

Emmie wiped her eyes with the back of her hand. "Or hear anything?"

"Only what you said. Why did you say Mary's name?"

Emmie swallowed. "Because she did it."

Sarah's mouth dropped open and she gasped. "How do you know?"

"Frankie just told me. He showed me, actually."

"I'm sorry, but who's Mary?" Finn asked.

"Frankie's mom," Emmie answered softly. "I can't believe I'm saying this, but she drowned him in this bathtub."

"You saw all of that just now?"

"Yes," she whispered.

Sarah turned Emmie around and nudged her toward the doorway. "Let's get out of here."

They stepped out of the bathroom and moved to the stairs. Emmie climbed slowly, like a delicate old woman who needed Sarah's support.

"Did you record any of it?" Emmie asked Finn as they got to the kitchen and he pulled a chair for her at the table.

He glanced at the camera in his hand. "The images I picked up on the thermal were far better than anything I've previously recorded. We can look at it together, if you'd like."

Emmie stared at the device. "I never expected this. Poor..." She paused. She was about to say *Poor Mary,* but the image of Mary pressing down Frankie's petite frame against the bottom of the bathtub rose in her mind. *Poor Frankie.* How could Mary have done something like that? Emmie sat heavy and still, sad and angry all at once.

It had always been poor Mary. Everyone had always said that. And all the time, she had murdered her own child.

Sarah shook her head, taking a chair next to Emmie's after putting a glass of water in front of her. "Why would she do something so horrible?"

"Frankie showed me The Lovers tarot card. I know now the number six on the ceiling referred to them—something to do with Mary's secret relationship with Robert. I was so blind I didn't see it before."

"Are you sure?"

"Frankie was clear this time. He *showed* me what happened in that bathtub. She did it on purpose. Cold, heartless murder." Her voice cracked. "He was taking a bath, and she held him under the water."

"But they found Frankie's body in the lake," Finn said. "You're the one who led them to his body, right?"

"Yes."

Finn moved in a little closer. "Wouldn't the autopsy show the cause of death? If his mother killed him here, the police would have known."

"It *is* all in the autopsy, but they didn't bother to search for the connection." Emmie gestured toward the basement. "She drowned him there, and that's why the water in his lungs had no debris from the lake. She held him down"—a sob tore through her, almost robbing her of all air—"and that's why that little boy had a bruise on his thorax. But they only interrogated Bobby Norris and then me and my family and put the case to rest."

"And Frankie never rested," Sarah said softly, looking around as if to find his spirit.

Emmie told Finn, "I just hope you recorded something we can use to prove all of this. She needs to pay for what she's done."

Finn lifted the device in his hands and stared into the display. After a few seconds of staring unblinkingly at the screen, the confused expression on his face transformed to shock.

"What's wrong?" Emmie asked.

"Nothing's wrong. I'm just stunned that I captured anomalies so well-defined. This is better than I had hoped for." He huddled closer and angled the screen so all of them could see it. He pointed to one of the forms. "This thing picks up thermal ranges from below zero Fahrenheit to hundreds of degrees. In this case, you can see the pockets of cold air."

A rainbow of colors shifted as patches of dark blue forms played out the same heart-wrenching murder scene Emmie had just witnessed. Finn had captured all of it on the device.

"That's it." Emmie pointed out the figures. "That's Mary and Frankie."

"Oh my God," Sarah said, "that's beyond awful."

"The police need to see this." Emmie's heart ached to watch it all again.

Finn groaned. "I hate to be the one to say it, but I doubt a judge would allow this sort of evidence."

Sarah shot back, "We can all see it."

Finn cleared his throat, looking annoyed. "I'll need to analyze it further before—"

"Hey guys." Emmie held up her hand. Finn was right. It would take more than this to catch Mary. "I need to make a call."

❧ 33 ❧

Emmie's whole being filled with pain as they watched the basement recording yet again, with John now at her side on the gnarly couch. Her eyes watered, but she held back the tears. It wouldn't help to break down crying in front of everyone.

John stared at the screen in silence as it played to the end. When it finished, he leaned back, expressionless, and Finn took the camera and switched it off. John turned to Emmie.

"You just recorded this now?"

"A little while ago."

"Things like this can be faked."

Finn pointed to the thermal camera in Emmie's hands, almost angry. "We didn't fake this. The three of us aren't in some pointless scheme together."

John shot Finn a restraining sideways glance.

Emmie's eyes held his. "Do you think I would accuse Mary of doing this for no reason, John? Mary, of all people? And a mother of killing her child?"

He shook his head. "I'm sure you wouldn't. But even if this is somehow the representation of something that happened—I don't know how, but I'll give you the benefit of the doubt because it's you—it's impossible to prove the figures in that video are Mary and Franklin. It's not proof, so what you think you saw doesn't matter in the eyes of the law."

She took his hands. "I know what I saw, John."

"Don't get me wrong—there's something there. I just don't know what. But you know how I feel about all this talk of ghosts."

"I know."

"Still..." He glanced at the thermal camera. "I don't understand how you were able to capture that."

"Mary did it. You—"

John held up his hand. "Wait, just listen. A mother killing her child isn't an accusation to be thrown about lightly. That's not a thing to say to a mother, and this is Mary you're talking about. What proof do you have?"

Emmie leaned forward. "But besides the video, it's everything you showed me in that folder this morning—no debris in the water, and the bruises. There wasn't any debris because Mary killed him here. She drowned him in the bathwater."

John winced, and his next question hung on his lips for a moment. "What motive would she have?"

"It has something to do with Robert."

"You think Robert is involved too?"

"I didn't see him there while she was killing Frankie or anything like that, but somehow Robert is connected." Emmie softened her tone. "Are you going to arrest her?"

The words hung in the air. John stood and paced the room, smoothing his shirt and shoving the ends further inside his pants as if trying to put order to a universe that had gone off its axis.

"I can't arrest Mary based on anything you've said so far. No evidence. Not even reasonable cause. I'd lose my badge."

Emmie's face hardened. "Show her the video. I know you don't believe in the paranormal, but she does. Make sure Robert is there with her, and after they see what we recorded, watch their reaction."

"She can just deny it and walk away."

"Maybe, but she knows what she did."

John paused as if deep in thought. "If it's true, a mother can't live with that guilt forever..."

"She quit church," Sarah said. "She said it the other day. I thought she meant she stopped believing after Frankie died, but maybe it was guilt."

"And I've got something else you can show her," Emmie said. "I found some of Frankie's old Murano marbles in the lake. Robert got them during a trip to Italy after his first wife's divorce, and he must have given them to Frankie as a gift when he returned. Some were also at Frankie's grave. How did they end up there? I'm thinking either Mary or Robert put them there, also out of guilt. Show them the video and show them the marbles."

Sighing, John glanced from the camera to Emmie. "I'm not so sure this will work. Or that it's a good idea."

Finn had been quiet, but he spoke up now. "I'm not sure I carry much weight here, but from what I've learned, you'll never get proof otherwise." Facing John, he nodded. "I think you know something happened. That it all fits now—and there is a woman who will get away with killing a little boy if you don't make her confess. You're a cop. You must have done it before."

John's eyes narrowed, then relaxed. He couldn't deny that he had interrogated suspects before. Emmie was proof of that after Frankie's death. She had once read that most murderers confessed during interrogations, at times even before being formally arrested. Hadn't they tried to make her confess to something she hadn't done? John threw her a mournful look, knowing that she still remembered those early interrogations, when he had been kind but firm, trying to find out the truth from her. He needed to do it to Mary now.

"You care for Mary, John," Emmie said gently, standing up to approach him. "You've known her a long time. So have I. But the truth is right here"—she pointed at the camera—"and we have to do something about it. Frankie deserves our help."

John's head swayed to the side and back as if fighting a mental argument. "She *was* lonely and overwhelmed, that's true..."

"Poor Mary, right?" Emmie said with a bitter, crooked smile.

John stared at the floor. "All right, I'll go out there."

"Thank you. I'll be right back." Emmie hurried upstairs and returned a minute later with a handful of multi-colored marbles. "Seven of them. Frankie was seven when he died."

Cupping his hands, John accepted the marbles. "I'll show her everything. I'll know what to do." He turned to Finn and narrowed his eyes. "If I find out later this is a hoax and you tricked her into believing—"

Emmie rested her hand on John's shoulder. "It's not like that, John. Trust me."

John gestured to Finn's camera. "Can I have that?"

Finn nodded and passed it to him. "Whatever you need."

"Stay here. All of you." John put his hand on Emmie's arm. "I'll let you know how it goes."

The three of them watched in silence as he headed out the door.

❧ 34 ❧

They sat at the kitchen table with the tarot cards in the center.

Emmie held her head in her hands. "What do you think they'll do to Mary if she confesses?"

"I'm not sure, but try not to think about it now," Sarah said. "If what you saw in the basement was the truth, then you're doing the right thing."

Taking a deep breath, Emmie looked over at a picture on the wall. Mary had put it up. They were standing together on the back steps, all of them except for Frankie, her parents and Mary by Emmie's side as if protecting her. Emmie's heart sank. *Not protecting me at all. Watching over me like a hawk, waiting to pounce at the first sign I'd figured out her game.*

"It all makes sense now..." Emmie said softly. "Mary was always asking me about Frankie, wondering if I'd ever heard from him or seen him or talked to him. She knew all about my gift, and she was trying to find out if I'd learned the truth yet. I can't believe I missed it before."

"At least you know what happened now. Not knowing is the worst thing, I think." Finn picked up the tarot cards and started to shuffle them like regular playing cards.

Emmie lurched over and grabbed them out of his hands. "Please don't do that! Not with those cards, anyway." She returned them to their box as she caught her breath.

"Oh, right, the *focus* cards." He nodded solemnly. "Sorry."

"I guess my nerves are a bit fried," she said.

"Mine too," Sarah said. She touched one of the two devices Finn had brought to the table. "What are these?"

He held up the one that looked like a camcorder. "This is my night vision camera. It didn't show anything out of the ordinary. I'll still analyze it when I get home, but I'm not hopeful." He held up the other one, which was like a gun. "This is my EMF, electromagnetic frequency device. I scanned the area during your encounter in the basement earlier and recorded some hot readings, but I couldn't run everything at once, so I focused on the thermal camera—fortunately."

Emmie turned the night vision camera to the side with her finger and read its manufacturer and model number. "You know a lot about the tech stuff."

Finn set down the EMF gun. "As it relates to the paranormal, anyway. I'm more interested in writing than technology. Learning to use all this stuff comes with the territory."

"Do you write about ghosts?" Sarah asked.

"Not yet. I'm a contributing editor for an online magazine called Cityscape. Mostly urban culture stories and local interests. Nothing earth-shattering. Ghost hunting fills my spare time."

Sarah nodded. "I've read it. So we won't end up in one of your stories?"

He gave her a smile as he threw a look at Emmie. "No. I promised."

Emmie looked toward the kitchen counter.

Sarah followed her gaze. "Can I get you something?"

"I'm thirsty," Emmie said.

"What kind of thirsty?" Sarah stood and pointed at the bottle of rum with one hand and at a glass of water with the other, as if she were shooting at both.

"I'd love the rum, actually," Emmie laughed. "But it's probably best to wait until after I've talked with John. He wouldn't appreciate having to explain what happened with Mary to a tipsy psychic."

Finn sneered a little. "What's up with him? Is he like your uncle or something?"

"Just a friend from way back."

"He looked like he wanted to tie me to the next rocket to the moon."

"He's just protective."

Finn scoffed. "He probably already ran a sample of my DNA by now."

Sarah smirked. "You worried about the results?"

"Nope. He can check me out. I don't have anything horrible to hide—just the normal stupid shit from my college years."

"What sort of stupid shit?" Emmie asked.

Finn rubbed his forehead. "Nothing too juicy, but never accept a stranger's party invitation on the other side of town if he's the one driving you there because it's a long walk home in the dark, and the police *might* stop you and ask why you're dressed in your underwear swinging a bottle of vodka."

Sarah grinned. "Sounds like a fun party."

"I don't remember a thing, except when they put me in the squad car. It's just best to stay away from too much alcohol."

"Good advice." Emmie glanced toward her bottle of rum on the counter again.

Sarah caught her staring and chuckled. "Just have one drink." She grabbed the bottle. "A little can't hurt, right?" She turned back to Finn. "Would you like some?"

Finn held up his hand. "None for me, thanks."

"Thank you, Sarah." Emmie slouched forward and gripped the pack of tarot cards in her hands. "Sorry, Finn, for putting you through all of this with me. Today hasn't gone anything like I expected."

"You have nothing to be sorry for." His eyes were gentle as he added, "You are trying to help others. And that's very often not easy."

Emmie noticed he moved between cynicism and sensitivity a lot. She looked at his electronics again. "What's your motivation for all of this? There's got to be *something* more to your hobby."

"Not really. Just passionate, innate curiosity."

She said nothing, just kept looking closely at him as Sarah got glasses from the cupboard.

He cleared his throat at her scrutiny, clearly unused to being on the receiving end of the questions. "I think everyone wonders what happens to us after we die."

"Is that really all it is?" she questioned. "All your dedication to this hobby? You're not looking to communicate with a dead loved one?"

Finn's gaze dropped to the table and he shrugged. *A-ha.*

Before he could say anything, the rum bottle cracked down against the countertop and Emmie spun around toward Sarah.

"Em," Sarah called. She had let go of the bottle and stood hunched forward, wincing, one hand clutching the edge of the counter. The blood had drained from her face. "I don't feel so good."

Emmie left her chair, rushed over, and held her up. "What's wrong?"

Sarah still cringed, as if someone were stabbing her. "I don't know. I feel weird."

Finn had also stood and pulled out his cellphone. "Should I call an ambulance?"

"Not yet." Sarah shivered. "Something passed through here, like when one of my patients dies. But this isn't the same thing." She disengaged gently from Emmie and stepped forward as if searching for something in the air. "This is a bad feeling, like something went horribly wrong."

They glanced around the room.

"Don't you feel it?" Sarah asked. "Something's going on."

A cool breeze passed over Emmie's face, then changed to bitter, freezing cold. "The Hanging Girl?"

"No. I don't think so. Not this time."

The room had cooled. A spirit was present, but who? Had the communication with the Hanging Girl and Frankie attracted an evil spirit? The cold air grew even more frigid and enveloped Emmie before thrusting her back against the wall like a blast from a gun. A chill hovered above her face, then swept down through her body. She screamed.

Finn's eyes grew wide. "What the hell's going on?"

"I don't know."

Emmie clutched the edge of the refrigerator and pulled herself forward toward the living room. She needed her phone. Sarah wobbled over to the kitchen counter, then followed her.

The three of them arrived in the living room just as one of the pictures on the wall crashed to the floor. Another dropped, then the rest. Glass scattered in every direction.

"Holy shit, what's happening?" Finn grabbed Emmie's outstretched hand.

The couch rumbled beside them moments before it slid across the room and thumped against the wall. Emmie's desk flipped upside down, throwing her laptop and lamp cracking to the floor. The bulb in the lamp exploded with a burst of sparks, then a puff of smoke.

"What the hell... what the hell..." Finn kept muttering, even as he tried to protect both women with his body.

He made them back away toward the front door. Another small flame erupted from one of the pictures that had dropped on the floor near the wall. Emmie rushed over and stomped on it to put out the fire. The photo showed Mary with her arm around Emmie as a young girl. Except that Emmie's face in the photo had been burned, but not anything else.

The truth hit Emmie, and she wavered, trying not to lose consciousness.

"Mary's here."

❧ 35 ❧

Sarah looked toward the front door. "Where?"

Emmie backed into the kitchen as her cellphone rang. John. She took a deep breath before answering it. "Hello?"

"I'm afraid I have some bad news," he said. "Are you sitting down?"

Her legs weakened. She leaned on the counter. "Yes. It's about Mary, isn't it?"

"I'm afraid so..." His voice came and went for a moment. "... is dead."

Emmie paused and went numb. "Dead?"

The reception was terrible. *He must still be at the farm.* "I'm so sorry. She... the recording... heard me and she just..."

She gripped her phone, as if that could make the words clearer. "The phone's cutting you off, John."

Something crashed into the living room wall. Emmie froze. Finn and Sarah huddled closer to her.

"Are you still there?" John's voice returned.

"Yes, John. Someone's entered the house. I know it's Mary."

"No, Emmie... misunderstood... *Mary is dead.*"

"Her spirit is here." Emmie glanced toward the kitchen. The pipes were rattling. "She's come back to hurt me. I know it."

"Sorry... I... hear you, either. Bad reception... guess... Mary impaled herself... and..."

The line died just as Finn stepped forward to examine the shattered picture on the floor. Then the side window in the living room imploded.

Glass sprayed over the floor around him. A couple of feet closer to the window and he would have borne the full brunt of the blast. He turned toward them. Blood covered his left arm and shards of glass stuck to his shirt and shorts.

"Damn!" Finn yelled.

Emmie threw the phone down and pointed at his arm. "Finn, you're bleeding!"

Sarah ran to him and checked the wounds. "Get over to the kitchen. I'll clean it up."

Finn followed Sarah. Banging and thumps swept across the house toward Mary's apartment. *Where the hell is she?* Emmie searched for any sign of Mary's spirit. No shadows, no forms. Nothing. But then, she had never seen an adult ghost.

"Mary is dead," Emmie said, running into the kitchen. "And she's here. That's what you felt, Sarah, but I can't see her."

Sarah was using wet paper towels to wipe off some blood along Finn's arm. They looked at Emmie, their faces full of shock in the stark light.

"I don't understand." Finn glanced around. "You mean her *spirit* is here?"

"Yes. From what I could make out, she might have committed suicide after John tried to question her. Can you still feel her?" Emmie asked Sarah.

Sarah shook her head, eyes wide, as she held on to Finn's arm. Splotches of blood dotted his skin. Then, gasping, Sarah closed her eyes for a moment. "I can feel her grief."

"Grief? Not anger?" Then it hit Emmie. *If Mary felt grief, then she wasn't after revenge...* "She's after Frankie."

"Why would she come after him?" Finn asked. "She *killed* him."

"All those photos of Frankie in her house, the marbles. Maybe it was true in some crazy way that she missed him..." Emmie eyed one of Finn's devices on the kitchen table. "I know she's here, but I can't see her. Can you help me find Mary with your electronics?"

"John has my thermal camera, but we can use the EMF." He picked up the smaller, gun-like device.

"I think she's over here." Emmie led Sarah and Finn back into the living room.

Someone pounded against the walls in Mary's apartment. Emmie charged toward the apartment door, but it slammed shut moments before she reached it.

As she gripped the door handle, a chill swept down her spine. She yanked on the door, but some unseen force held it shut until finally it opened as if she were prying apart two powerful magnets. *Nothing inside.* She turned to Sarah. "Do you sense anything?"

Sarah nodded and held her stomach. "I'm freezing, and I feel nauseous again."

"That's got to be her."

Finn stepped forward and scanned the room with his device. "High readings straight ahead."

Emmie squinted into the empty space and focused. Still no form, but a strange, high-pitched squeal formed at the top range of her hearing before dropping down to a menacing growl.

Then the sudden scream: "You betrayed me!"

It was Mary's voice, loud and clear.

"I didn't." Emmie winced at the emotional pain welling up inside her. "*You* killed Frankie! Why?"

"I hate you!" Mary screamed again, and again the room flooded with cold air as if someone had opened a freezer.

A patch of air darkened several feet ahead, like a storm cloud blocking the sun. A brief shadow revealed Mary's outline and burning black eyes. Blood drained from a wound on Mary's chest. She glared at Emmie.

Emmie stepped back as Mary's spirit took shape. This was not another pleading child, this was a raging woman—her first adult spirit. The sight jarred her senses. Why now? What had changed?

I'm not afraid of her anymore.

Emmie moved forward. "How could you do that to your son?"

Eyes full of anger but also pain stared back. "I had no choice! Who was there to help me raise him? Nobody. The only man who cared for me refused to accept him. Even Frankie's father didn't want him. No one wanted my Frankie. I couldn't take care of him alone anymore. I did the only thing I could do. I was his mother, and I took care of him."

"How can you say such a thing? We were there! We helped you!"

"Poor Mary, poor Mary, poor Mary, poor Mary," she said until the words blended together. She let out an anguished wail. "You think I couldn't hear your parents all the time? And John, when he was here? And the other mothers at school? Poor Mary, poor Mary, poor Mary!"

"Stop," Emmie commanded. Sarah's hand took hers. Sarah wasn't looking at the right spot—she couldn't see Mary—and Finn could only point where his devices led him. Could they hear her?

Mary's voice filled with melancholy. "I was just a child when I gave birth, lonely and working all the time. But my parents didn't want me back. No man wanted me, except married men, to pass the time." A smile like a horrible grimace spread on her face. "But Robert wanted me." The smile became even more horrible as she shrugged and added, "He just didn't want Frankie."

The live woman and the dead one faced each other. Mary swayed, certain of her reasons, and Emmie felt the tears well in her eyes and stream down her face.

"You killed Frankie so you could be with Robert?" she asked in a whisper.

"Poor Mary, poor Mary," Mary said, still swaying. "Alone for years and years, all her youth going, and the man who loves her going because he doesn't want a new son when his own son is dead."

It was too horrible to contemplate. "He told you to kill Frankie?"

"No!" Mary screamed. And in a softer voice, she added, "He never knew until tonight." Another noise like a growl came from her. "You... *you* ruined everything. You betrayed me and stole Robert from me. I saw the disgust on his face! So now I'm taking Frankie back."

"You can't take him."

Sarah squeezed her hand and said in a low voice, "We won't let her."

Mary sneered. "He's all mine now. I won't be lonely again."

Her form flared, then faded away.

"I lost the signal." Finn adjusted his device.

Emmie pressed her eyes closed and focused on Frankie. She needed to find him before Mary did. "I have to warn Frankie."

"All right, I've got a new signal," Finn said. "Something's moving down through the floor into the basement. If that's a spirit, its signature is strong."

"I can't let Mary get to him before I do," Emmie said.

She opened her eyes, turned, and whizzed past Finn and Sarah, circling around through the kitchen and stomping down the basement stairs. The others followed her.

Emmie flipped on the lights at the bottom of the steps and scrambled through the basement. No sign of Mary. She asked Finn, "Do you see anything?"

He checked his EMF device, turning back toward the laundry room. "Lots of mixed signals down here. Maybe the bad wiring?"

Hide, Frankie. Stay away from your mom.

"Do you want me to get the tarot cards from upstairs?" Sarah asked.

"No." *Can't use them this time.* If she used The Tower card again to summon Frankie, the Hanging Girl wouldn't miss the opportunity to attack her through the open channel.

Finn pointed to the far side of the basement. "Something's very strong over there."

Emmie squeezed her eyes shut and focused on Frankie. *You got this, Em.*

The chilling cries of children enveloped her senses as she tuned her senses to the spirit realm.

Meditate and communicate.

It didn't take long before they appeared. All the same children who'd approached her before—but now, instead of a dozen, at least thirty flooded in. Each of them called to her and pleaded to tell their stories. No time to hear their tales now.

She strained to find Frankie. "Where are you, Frankie? Your mom is in the house, but don't go near her. Do you hear me? Stay away from your mom now. Just hide, Frankie."

Tears streamed from Emmie's eyes. She opened them, but the spirits still surrounded her. Finn and Sarah moved through them without noticing.

Frankie was nearby.

"Hide, Frankie!" Emmie shouted.

Soft footsteps scurried away. It had to be him. *Good, Frankie. Stay hidden and don't come out.*

Several other child spirits blocked his location, and no sign of the Hanging Girl. Not yet, anyway. No way to see beyond them. So many, and more on the way.

"Help me! Hide Frankie from his mom." Emmie yelled at the spirits, but their own cries for help rose above her own.

Sarah moaned and folded forward. "She's here." Her face had turned pale again.

"Over there!" Finn gestured toward the bathroom door. "Very strong signal now."

"That's her." Emmie rushed to the bathroom and flung open the door. Icy air poured out as she stepped inside. Panic rushed through her chest.

Emmie shuddered at the sight of Mary's dark form embracing Frankie in the bathtub. One hand covered his eyes, and the other his mouth.

"You did this!" Mary screamed. Her blackened form shifted and pulsed as Frankie squirmed to get away. Her empty black eyes burned with hatred.

Frankie broke free for a moment, crying out in pain, but she smothered him again as his spirit weakened within hers.

"Let him go, Mary." Emmie reached for him. "He's suffered so much."

"No!" she screamed. "He's coming with me."

Two spirits of children approached Emmie again, and she turned her attention to them. "Please help me get that boy away from her. Pull her away from him. Can you help me?"

They stared at the scene in the bathtub but made no motion to help. Instead, they pleaded for help themselves, begging Emmie to take them home while crowding in closer to her.

Emmie reached further toward Frankie, grabbing at him, her hands passing through his spirit.

Mary swatted at her arms. "You did this to us! He's mine, you won't have him!"

The intersection of their bodies sent an icy electric pulse surging through Emmie. She waved her hands through Frankie's body as if he might somehow feel her energy and move toward her.

"You've got to get away from her, Frankie." Emmie reached in again as Mary pulled him back. Frankie's bright, warm spirit darkened and cooled.

She touched something. Frankie's leg? She connected with him for a moment. Her energy touched his spirit. Just a little more, and she could pull him away. Her fingers grasped strands of energy, lumps of invisible flesh. The connection stretched away as Mary pulled him with her.

"I won't let you go, Frankie." Emmie focused again, this time straining her mind while grabbing at his torso. He was there in her hands, and she pulled at whatever link held them together. Just a thin, weak bond, but she clung to him with all her strength.

Mary yanked him back, surrounding Frankie's spirit as Emmie took swipes at her twisted form, but they had no effect.

You can't stop her, Em.

"Help me!" Emmie yelled again to the surrounding spirits.

"How can we help you?" Sarah stretched her arms into the tub.

"Pull him," Emmie said.

Mary lurched back, sinking Frankie further into the darkness of her being.

"Come back to me, Frankie," Emmie said, speaking to one and then to the other. "Mary, please let him go. You can't leave me again, Frankie. Let him go and have peace."

Frankie's called out weakly before he broke free from Mary's grasp. Emmie's grip on his leg slipped away as he lurched from the tub and ran from the room faster than she'd ever seen him run.

"Yes, Frankie, go hide! We'll play a game now. Hide in the best place you can find. I'll come looking for you."

A burst of cold air swept through Emmie as Mary screamed. Emmie stumbled back into Finn's arms for a moment before she hit the ground.

The lights went out.

❧ 36 ❧

"Not now!" Emmie's eyes slowly adjusted to the darkness. The digital screen on Finn's device became their only light until they each pulled out a cellphone to use as flashlights.

Sarah held out her cellphone toward the tub. "Did she do that to the lights?"

"Maybe, but more likely it's the Hanging Girl."

Sarah's eyes widened above her cellphone screen. "Mary's furious. She's running away."

"We have to get to Frankie before she does."

Finn pointed to the ceiling. "The signal is moving up through the floor again."

They hurried out of the bathroom to the bottom of the staircase. No time to reset the breaker.

Sarah squeezed Emmie's arm. "I feel sick again."

Emmie put her arm around Sarah's back. "Just hang in there. She can't..." She stopped herself. *She can't hurt you? Is that what I was going to say?* Her mom's words came back, but they weren't true anymore. "She can't... *stop* us. Frankie is hiding somewhere. Probably in his old room."

Finn rushed up the stairs. "There's more activity up here."

Emmie and Sarah followed and nearly crashed into him as he halted in the doorway leading into the kitchen.

"What's wrong?" Emmie peered around him. Someone had scattered all the tarot cards from the table across the kitchen floor. Every card faced down except one. The Tower.

"Someone was here." Finn tiptoed around the cards.

"It's Frankie, and I know where he's hiding." Emmie rushed through the kitchen. "Follow me."

They crossed the living room into Mary's old apartment. No need to check Frankie's old bedroom anymore—he wasn't there.

Finn glanced into the bedrooms anyway, with his device held out in front of him. "A strong signal in this area."

Sarah's face was queasy again.

"Mary's in here looking for him." Emmie paused and stared back at Sarah and Finn. "It's going to get worse, I think, when she can't find him. Frankie's hiding out where his old treehouse used to be. The Hanging Girl might be with him too."

"What can we do?" Sarah asked.

Emmie ran her fingers through her hair, trying to think. "He's trapped, but if I can get him away from here, his spirit can move on."

Finn stared at his device. "I've never seen a signal this high. It's right here..." He stretched out his hand toward Mary's old bedroom doorway. He shuddered, then lurched backward. "Dammit! Something shocked me."

Sarah nodded, holding her stomach. "She's so angry. I feel like she wants to rip me apart."

"We better get out there." Emmie headed toward the back door. "It won't take her long to find him."

They hurried outside. Thunder cracked nearby as dark clouds covered the sky.

Heaving in a deep breath, Sarah looked up. "It'll rain soon."

Emmie led them toward the Hanging Tree. "It won't take long. I can get to him first. I'm sure of it."

Sarah gulped in a few more deep breaths as they hurried

across the lawn toward the back of the garage. Another thunder cloud rumbled.

A cold intensity spread across Emmie as she caught sight of the Hanging Tree. She paused. Sarah and Finn stopped a few steps later.

The Hanging Girl was there, pulling herself up the rope with the noose still wrapped around her throat. Frankie sat on the branch above her, where his old treehouse had been long ago. She inched toward him, glancing back at Emmie with that same disturbing grin.

"You're too late." The Hanging Girl wheezed in a laugh.

"Frankie," Emmie said, "get out of the tree now. Come over to me."

"You found me too fast." Frankie chuckled. "You cheated."

Emmie shook her head. "You left me a good clue, Frankie. But the game's over and you need to come down now. They want to hurt you."

"Alice won't hurt me." Frankie watched the Hanging Girl climb higher and throw her arms over the main branch. She pulled herself up only a couple feet from Frankie now. "She's my friend. She protects me."

"From who?"

Frankie lost his grin. "Everyone. But she likes to play games."

"No more games, Frankie. Get away from her. She's tricking you."

The Hanging Girl gazed at Emmie with those same wide, protruding bug eyes. "He's mine."

Emmie stepped closer. "You've been hiding him, haven't you?"

The Hanging Girl's legs dangled from the branch, her white nightgown swaying in the opposite direction from the growing wind. "His mother abandoned him. He's mine. The house is mine."

"He needs to come with me before his mother gets back. Frankie," Emmie raised her voice, "please come down here."

The Hanging Girl nudged in closer to Frankie, stroking his hair with her hands of sickly, pale flesh. "He's not going anywhere."

Finn approached the tree, aiming his device at the branch. "Two strong signals. Damn, I wish I could see them."

"No, you don't..." Emmie whispered.

Sarah also moved closer to where Frankie sat. Her eyes watered. "That's Frankie, isn't it? He's *right there*." She pointed at him. "A beautiful spirit."

"Still a powerful signal in that direction." Finn scanned the area back toward the house with his device.

The Hanging Girl embraced Frankie, slipping one forearm over his throat as she grinned at Emmie. "Leave us alone."

"Play with us, Emmie!" Frankie called out as the Hanging Girl's grip tightened. "It's my turn. Go hide, and I'll find you."

The Hanging Girl slapped her hand over his mouth. "I don't like that. You can't play with us. Go away!"

Not going away.

Emmie crept closer, the girl's eyes beaming down on her. Shards of old wood remained in the place where steps had once led to the treehouse's door. Emmie clung to the side of the tree, then pulled herself up onto the first step. The wood creaked as her shoe scraped across the bark. "Come over here, Frankie. Move away from her before your mom gets here."

The Hanging Girl laughed. "She can't have him either. He's mine forever. Forever and ever!"

Emmie rose to the next step, reaching out toward Frankie's leg.

The Hanging Girl sneered and pulled Frankie closer.

From the third step, Emmie strained toward Frankie, this time running her fingertips across something that reminded her of a science-class experiment with electricity. The tingling sensation of touching a plasma ball. He was there, within reach, but pulling on him was like trying to grasp a wisp of smoke.

Emmie clawed at his form. "Frankie, your mom will be here

soon, and she'll take you away from me and everybody else. She'll try to take you to a horrible place. You can't go with her, do you understand?"

The girl still covered his mouth. He nodded.

"I need you to move away from her too." Emmie gestured toward the girl, staring into her eyes without flinching.

Frankie didn't move.

"You can't take him," the Hanging Girl mocked, then erupted in a shrieking laughter. She stretched out her hand toward Emmie's throat. "Just a little closer and I'll consume your last breath. Please, oh please, just a little closer."

Emmie's mind went back to the bedtime prayer. "Now I lay me down to sleep, I pray the Lord my soul to keep. If I should die before I wake, I pray the Lord my soul to take."

The Hanging Girl's eyes glossed over, and her sneer faded as if she were caught in a trance.

Emmie repeated the line again and again, pulling at Frankie's spirit. There *had* to be a way to get him out of there. The girl's grip around his neck didn't loosen.

"Go away," the girl muttered, as if on the edge of sleep.

Emmie moved closer to Frankie, reaching toward his face. His blue eyes and light-brown hair—just like she remembered.

The girl's own eyes softened, just a bit.

"You know that prayer, don't you?" Emmie gazed at the girl's outstretched hand, following her slender fingers to their tips. Dirt and broken nails.

The Hanging Girl snarled. "Go away. My house."

"You're not a monster. You're Alice Hyde. I know who you are, and I know that you died here by hanging in 1921, either by suicide or murder."

"I'm not dead. Do I *look* dead?"

"Did someone kill you? Do you remember what happened?"

"I wasn't hanged in any tree. I come and go as I please. You're blind and a Dumb Dora."

"You're dead. A long time ago you were hanged here, and you've terrorized me all my life."

"Of course I have. You won't get out of my house. It's mine! You should be the one hanging from this tree for trying to steal my home."

"Who did this to you? Who hanged you?"

The girl looked down. "Do you see anyone hanging beneath this branch?"

Emmie pointed to the noose around the girl's neck. "What's that then? You always have a noose around your neck everywhere you go."

"What? This?" The girl pulled at it. "My necklace, and I can take it off anytime I want. Those Reubens failed to steal my house."

"Who failed?"

The Hanging Girl trembled as if about to explode with anger. "I don't want to talk to you anymore. You're wasting my time. And the boy's mom will arrive shortly." She pulled Frankie to her. "She can't have him either."

His eyes drooped, and he mumbled with the girl's hand still over his mouth.

Emmie told the girl, "Let him talk."

"He's said too much already. Silence is golden."

"You silenced him for years, haven't you? You hid him away from me so I couldn't find him, right? So you could have him all to yourself."

The girl's hideous grin widened. "He's mine, but I still let him play hide and seek with you sometimes. I warned him the Dumb Dora wouldn't play with him anymore, but he didn't believe me. What did you do? You didn't play with him." The girl laughed. "He called for you to find him so many times. He waited and waited, and just gave up."

"I didn't know," Emmie said mournfully.

"Blind and stupid. He's better off with me."

Sarah said, "Something's wrong, Em."

Emmie looked down.

Finn gestured toward the house. "The numbers are off the charts."

"Please, Alice, let him go," Emmie pleaded with the girl once more. "I have to get him out."

"It's too late, anyway. The mother is here. We'll see how *she* does at hide and seek."

❧ 37 ❧

Emmie adjusted her eyes to the warping shadow of a figure near the edge of the garage. Mary—blood-red eyes, veins pulsing in her eyeballs. Her blonde hair now matted, and her warm smile erased. The vague silhouette faded in and out as it approached.

A thick dark cloud floated behind Mary, following at the same pace, and Emmie spotted the connection between them when they came closer. A slender thread, like an umbilical cord, running from the murky depths to the back of Mary's head. The cloud's outer fog revealed a black interior, and Mary pulled against it relentlessly, as if on the verge of escaping its grasp. The darkness swarmed and shifted in place like an impatient pet awaiting instructions.

Finn faced Mary, his device pointed at her spirit and companion as if he could see them. He stepped forward.

Emmie tensed. *Careful, Finn. If you only knew what you've gotten yourself into.*

It looked as if they might collide until Finn moved off to the side at the last second. His eyes widened and his mouth dropped open. "I wish I had my thermal camera."

Emmie turned to Frankie one last time before climbing down and meeting his eyes. "I won't let anyone take you, Frankie."

The Hanging Girl still held on to him.

Emmie dropped onto the grass as Mary moved within several feet of her.

Sarah stepped in beside Emmie, holding out her hand toward Mary. "Her pain and anger—they're overwhelming. I can hardly stand it." Sarah winced.

Mary called to Frankie—not in her usual sweet tone. Now she spoke between gasps for air and each word spilled out through mouthfuls of blood. "Get down from there." She sneered at the Hanging Girl and Emmie. "What have you done to my boy?"

"Frankie loved you, Mary," Emmie said, trying to control her emotion.

For a moment, Mary's red eyes faded back to blue. "I loved him too."

"You were mad, then." Emmie shook her head. "You must have been."

"I did what I had to do, for love. To have a life, not that horrible purgatory!" Mary's eyes glossed over, then burned red again. "But you ruined everything. All I worked for, you destroyed. Robert looking at me as if I were the devil. For so many years, he loved me!"

Mary charged at Emmie, hitting into her like a bag of ice as Mary's fingers tore at Emmie's neck. Mary's breath blasted arctic air across Emmie's face.

Sarah reached into the space Mary occupied and closed her eyes for a moment. Mary convulsed and staggered back as Emmie toppled over across the grass.

Dropping beside her, Sarah panted.

"What did you do?"

"I tried to help her."

"Like you do for the patients?"

Sarah nodded. "She doesn't want my help."

"She won't leave without Frankie."

"Emmie, you're bleeding," Finn said, crouching by her and reaching toward her neck.

Emmie touched the crawling warmth there. The blood trickled down the side of her fingers as she looked at them.

The dark form behind Mary grew larger and floated along as Mary moved up the tree toward Frankie.

"Come here, Frankie." Mary reached the branch and stretched toward him. "Mommy still loves you."

The Hanging Girl laughed. "You have a funny way of showing it." Frankie cowered behind the Hanging Girl. "He doesn't want to play right now."

Mary inched up. "It's time to go, sweetheart."

"Yes, it's time for you to go." The Hanging Girl pulled off her noose and tossed it over Mary's neck.

Mary struggled to remove it as the Hanging Girl thrust her off the branch and Mary fell, along with her dark counterpart. The rope tightened until her neck cracked and her body recoiled.

The Hanging Girl laughed. "My tree!"

"Mommy!" Frankie cried out, reaching toward Mary. "Let her go!"

"Don't bother, boy, she's better off like that."

Mary swayed back and forth on the rope, kicking and struggling while reaching up to Frankie. "Help me, my little man. You can't leave me to die here."

The Hanging Girl groaned. "You stuck your fingers in his mouth so he couldn't scream while you drowned him." She grinned at Mary while holding Frankie back. "You abandoned him and now you need his help? Much too late."

Frankie rushed around the Hanging Girl and clung to his mother's blood-drenched shirt. The rope slipped off Mary's neck and she dropped to the ground, pulling Frankie down with her. Her face contorted as she gathered Frankie into her arms, smothering him as the dark form behind her moved in and started merging with Mary's and Frankie's spirits.

"Mary, let him go!" Emmie struggled forward on hands and knees and tugged at Frankie's arm.

Mary snarled. "This is all your fault. You did this to us."

"No, never to him."

"Your fault." Mary's back faded into the cloudy darkness.

Emmie called to Sarah. "Can you grab his hand?"

"I don't see him." She rushed to Emmie and reached through Frankie's space. "Yes, I feel him. I'll try."

Emmie's grip on Frankie's arm loosened as the darkness swallowed more of Mary. "Finn, pull me back."

Letting go of his device, Finn grabbed her around the waist and dragged her back a few inches.

Beyond the Hanging Tree, several children appeared in the background. They watched Emmie struggle and still pleaded for her help.

"You," Emmie called to them, "help this boy!"

The Hanging Girl chuckled from the branch. "Why should they help you?"

"You know what it is to be lost! Please, help me save my friend."

The children crowded in closer now, pointing out their wounds to Emmie.

She yanked at Frankie with all her strength but kept her eyes on the children. "I see all of you. I promise I'll help you this time. Things will be different from now on, I promise. I just need to get him away from her."

Boys and girls, some in torn jeans and t-shirts, and some in dresses from decades earlier, all approached Emmie. A few grabbed Frankie at first, then more. They told her their stories even as they pulled.

Frankie emerged from Mary's grasp little by little. He glanced back at his mother. "Emmie, I'm scared."

"Don't look at her."

They stretched Frankie back and forth like in a tug of war.

"He's mine!" Mary shrieked.

The Hanging Girl dropped from her branch and joined the other children. She leaned in next to Emmie and with combined strength they loosened Mary's hold on Frankie. One by one, the children peeled Mary's fingers from his body.

A low moaning erupted from the cloudy darkness consuming Mary. One low voice cried out, then more. A multitude of screams swelled, like those of terrified victims falling through an endless void as the mass encompassed her body. The blackness churned, oozing over her face and neck. The stench of rotten eggs filled the air.

She had lost Frankie, and now the cloudy black form devoured Mary, her eyes wide and her teeth clenched until she disappeared.

❧ 38 ❧

Frankie faced Emmie as Mary faded away into the blackness. Emmie reached out and held his hand, connecting with his fragile energy bristling at the edge of her fingertips. His eyes sparkled and strands of his light-brown hair waved as if the gusts of wind from the incoming storm affected him.

Sarah moved closer to Frankie and gasped. "She's gone, isn't she?"

"Yes."

The Hanging Girl backed away, standing among the other children with her eyes fixed on Frankie.

Finn rested his hand on Emmie's shoulder. "You okay?"

"Time to say goodbye to him." She gestured to Frankie.

"I wish I could see him." Finn strained his eyes at the space in front of Emmie.

The children closest to Emmie, a gaunt young boy wearing ragged clothes and a tall red-haired girl of about twelve moved back as Emmie knelt in front of Frankie. She rested her palm against his cheek. So pure. The cuts and bruises were gone. Nothing remained of the horrible trauma he'd been through.

"It's okay if you want to move on now," Emmie said,

"although I'm not exactly sure how to do that. I've never helped anyone do that before."

Frankie smiled. "I feel better now, but I feel strange." He furrowed his brow and looked down at himself.

Sarah held out her hand toward him. "Maybe I can help. Guide me to his head." She moved her hand over his hair.

"You're right there," Emmie said.

Following the curve of his forehead, Sarah's hand moved down. "He has a lot of energy, and it's getting stronger." She stopped on a spot a few inches above his right ear.

Frankie's eyes fluttered as if he were going into a hypnotic state.

"This is just how it feels at the hospital right before a patient passes away." Sarah beamed and nodded. "His essence is here. It's like a feather-light balloon, and I just need to... let it go..."

"Wait, Sarah." Emmie clung to Frankie's shifting energy. She held back her tears, but her voice was a little garbled. "I'll miss you, Frankie."

"I'll miss you too, Emmie." His gaze met hers, then he smirked. "What card do I have in my pocket?"

Emmie grinned. "You want to play a game now?"

"Just try to guess the card, goofy."

"You don't have a card in your pocket, Frankie."

He laughed. "I tried to trick you. You're right, I don't have any cards left. But I hid a card in your bedroom. Don't guess it now, okay? Don't cheat! Wait until you go to bed before looking for it."

"I won't cheat," she promised softly.

"I know. You've never cheated, I know that."

Sarah looked at Emmie. "Ready?"

"Yes." Emmie nodded once. "Later, Frankie."

Frankie's face glowed before his body dissolved into a silhouette of light. A flash of warmth flowed through Emmie's fingers as he faded and rose into the air above the tree. Lightning flashed between the thundering clouds overhead, and he disappeared.

The Hanging Girl and the other children were silent in that moment as Emmie stood up, still following Frankie with her eyes although he was gone. She took her fingers to her lips and blew him a kiss.

She sighed. Despite the Hanging Girl's help against Mary, it was difficult to meet her bully face to face. The chill of childhood memories still clutched her insides. Her muscles tensed. That twisted girl's face had haunted her childhood and terrorized her.

But Emmie finally turned to the children.

The Hanging Girl spoke first. "You took away my friend."

"He was my friend too. But he needed freedom, and we have a lot to talk about."

"You never listened to me before. Why should I trust you?"

"Because I'm ready to listen, and I can help you, just like I helped Frankie."

It took a moment for the girl to say, "You won't like what I have to say."

"I have no doubt about that."

Sarah touched Emmie's shoulder. "Is there another spirit needing help? Maybe I can do the same thing for them? Judging by the bitterness in the air, I think you're talking to the Hanging Girl, right? I can help her move on too."

The girl stepped back. "I'm not leaving my house. I don't need your help."

"Wouldn't you like us to release you from this world?" Emmie asked.

"No. This is my house and don't try any of your tricks on me. I've been watching you for years, and I won't play any of your games. You want me to leave, I know it, so you can have the house all to yourself. You want to steal it from me."

Emmie shook her head. "We can share it."

The Hanging Girl laughed. "Share my house? I don't need guests."

"I want to know what happened to you."

The Hanging Girl's lips formed a ghoulish grin. "I'll tell you my story. A rude family and their Dumb Dora daughter tried to steal my house, but I killed them all. How do you like that ending? I can make it come true."

"Threats won't help. We can talk about why you always wear that noose around your neck."

The noose materialized around the Hanging Girl's neck with the other end of the rope now strung up around the branch. The girl reached behind her head and ran her fingers over the knot. "It can't stop me."

"Who did that to you?" Emmie asked again.

A confused look passed over the Hanging Girl's face for a moment before reverting to a sneer. "I won."

"I'd love to know what happened, but I have nowhere else to go. If you allow me to share the house with you, I promise I'll help you as much as I can."

"I don't need your help. I can take care of myself."

"That might be true, but maybe we can share this space." Emmie glanced back at the house. The idea of sharing it with Bug Eyes didn't appeal to her either, but she wouldn't just pack up her things and abandon the place now. There had to be *something* she could offer the girl. Something to keep the peace. Something the girl would appreciate. "That music box I have in my room, did that belong to you? Those are your initials carved into the side, right? AH—Alice Hyde? My dad found it in the attic."

The girl narrowed her eyes. "It's mine. He stole it from me."

Emmie nodded. "I'm sure he didn't know it was yours. It's a beautiful toy. The song is lovely."

"You can't have it."

"Did you keep your jewelry in it?"

The girl groaned. "No."

"As a child, I used to open that music box before bed and let the song play to keep you away. Do you remember that? You left me alone after I played it. Why?"

"Because it's my song."

"I can play it every night before bed for you."

"I can listen to it anytime I want."

"I don't think you can. I've never heard you play it in all the years I've lived here. But I can do that for you. I think you like that song, right?"

"Yes."

"I'll play it every night for you, but we need to call a truce. I can't go on like this. Please let me share the house with you."

The Hanging Girl grumbled, "It's my house, but you can stay for now."

"Thank you." Emmie stared into the eyes of the other children. "And thank you for helping me save my friend. I'll listen to all your stories and help as much as I can. I just need some time."

A police siren blared in the distance. John would be there soon.

What took you so long, John?

Probably better he hadn't shown up earlier, anyway. He would have thought she'd gone completely nuts.

"I won't let you down," she promised the children.

39

E mmie just wanted a glass of water as they crossed through the house toward the front door. John pounded on the door, but they couldn't get there before he rushed inside with his hand on the pistol in his holster. He held an object in his other hand.

John surveyed the area and eyed Finn first, then focused on Emmie. "Are you safe?"

"Yes, now we are."

"What happened?"

"It was Mary. I know that's not what you want to hear, but it's true."

John stepped carefully over the broken glass and scanned the floor. "All of this happened right about the time I called you?"

"Yes."

Glass crunched beneath his shoes. "A lot of damage here. Did you see anyone outside? Any kids running away?"

"No. Nothing like that, John."

The shattered picture frames lay on the floor. John stopped above the one with her face burned out. "Someone start a fire?"

Emmie shook her head. *Mary's fury.*

John pointed to it. "How the hell did that happen?"

Emmie gazed at Sarah, and then Finn. "It's hard to explain."

John shot her a sideways glance. "I see. Another paranormal event?"

"Yes."

He turned to them. "It's an old house. A sudden change in air pressure could have blown out the glass, especially with the storm coming in. Or a flock of birds flying too low—some of them could have gotten disorientated and hit the glass. That happens all the time, you know."

"Nothing like that this time, John." *If only you'd been here to see it happen.*

"We'll see. Check outside your windows tomorrow. I'll bet you find some dead birds lying on the ground."

No point in explaining further. Emmie went to the kitchen and poured herself a glass of water. Sarah stayed close to her side, with Finn backing away against the counter as John stood between them.

John lifted the object in his hand. Finn's thermal camera. Now just a pile of broken plastic, wires, and a cracked screen, he passed it to Finn. "Sorry, Mr. Adams, but Mary, the suspect, smashed it on the ground during her arrest."

Finn stared at the mess. "I guess it's nothing compared to everything else that happened tonight." He pensively turned it over in his hands.

"What happened at the farm, John?" Emmie asked. It was better to know.

John turned, his joyless eyes focused on her. "When I arrived at Mary's house, I showed her and Robert the recording and the marbles. She panicked. It was like she already knew you'd seen Frankie. She broke down in tears and spilled everything. She admitted to killing Frankie after Robert refused to marry anyone with children. I guess it was too much for her to handle after all the troubles in her life. Robert was just as shocked as anyone.

Before I could get close to her, she ran and grabbed a bayonet from an old musket off the wall in the living room. She charged out the back door with it. I chased after her, but before we could stop her, she threw herself on it in the back lawn. Pierced her own heart."

Emmie covered her heart and closed her eyes for a moment. A cloud of sadness weighed on her. She leaned into John and hugged him. "If only I could have done something more to prevent all this."

John patted her back. "She made those evil choices. Nothing you could have done differently."

Emmie squeezed him before backing away. "It's hard for me to believe that."

"Robert is in shock about all this. I don't think he believed a woman could do something like that to her child because of something he said. But neither you nor him should think this is somehow your somehow your fault."

Emmie nodded slowly. "Mary wasn't... well."

"Yes. You should have seen how she cracked after seeing those marbles." His eyes were haunted for a second, although he had seen no ghosts. "Good thing you found them, as they proved to be the last straw for her."

Emmie stared at the floor. "I know I'm supposed to feel happy for Frankie now, but I feel rotten instead."

"The whole thing was rotten, Emmie." John stepped closer. "But if she was dropping those marbles at his grave and filling her house with his photos, I suspect she would only have been at peace when her crime was known."

"And I need to do more for the other children too."

"What other children?" John asked.

Emmie looked into his eyes. "We can talk more about that later."

"All right," John said. "And I should probably mention that after Mary's confession about Frankie, I can't promise investigators won't ask to come in with more questions. They screwed up the first time, and the case is going to have to be re-opened and re-closed."

"That's okay, I understand." She gave a small, sad smile. "At least they won't think it was me this time."

A quiet moment passed between them. *Quiet.* The pipes no longer banged against the kitchen floor. Only the refrigerator hummed.

John stepped back toward the door. "You're welcome to stay in our guest room for the night if it would help. I'm sure my wife wouldn't mind a little company with the empty nest now. You know how she *loves* to talk."

Emmie smiled warmly and followed John as he headed for the door. "I think I'll be okay. I'd rather sleep in my bed tonight."

They gathered in front of the door. John looked from each of them to the other, ending with Emmie. "I'll just head home then. Call me if you need anything, okay?"

"I will."

John's foot crunched onto a piece of glass. He lifted his shoe and picked it off, carrying it with him outside. "You should throw some plastic over those windows in case it rains, although I think the storm's headed north of here. Keep the bugs out, anyway."

"Got it, and I'll close my bedroom door."

"Take care, Emmie." John turned and left.

Over the next hour, they worked together to patch up the windows with garbage bags and duct tape. No talk of ghosts or Mary or Frankie. Hardly any talk at all—too exhausted.

On the way out to his car, Finn gestured to his broken thermal camera. "It was worth it."

"I'm glad I met you when I did."

"If you need any more help..."

"I will, probably sooner than you think."

Finn smiled. "I'm always up for it."

With his car loaded, he shared goodbyes with her and Sarah in the driveway and took off down the street.

Sarah hugged Emmie a moment later. "If you need some company, I wouldn't mind sleeping on the couch. You've been through a lot."

Funny how it felt like they'd been friends forever. "Nobody deserves to sleep on that horrible thing." Emmie chuckled. "And I've got Alice inside to keep me company, remember?"

"Do you think she'll ever leave?" Sarah glanced at the house.

"Maybe she doesn't need to."

After Sarah left, Emmie stood in the driveway alone as the thunder rumbled overhead. The wind intensified and ruffled through her hair. A darkened silhouette of a girl stood in the window of Emmie's parents' old bedroom. The Hanging Girl—no, *Alice*. Emmie took a deep breath and waved. The girl faded back into the shadows.

No need to run anymore, but so many things to do. So many voices to be heard.

She walked back inside and cleaned the living room a little before heading up to her bedroom.

With her back to the door, she listened to footsteps bump across the wood floor as someone approached. They stopped in her doorway. She didn't turn around.

"Alice, I'll play it for you," Emmie said. "Just like I said. Every night."

She caught sight of the music box next to her bed and opened it to start the old, tinny music. "O Sole Mio." A sweet, soothing sound.

Alice was silent.

Emmie left her light on as Alice still stood in her doorway. It would take time to get used to the change.

Frankie's words flashed through her mind and she reached under her pillow. Her fingers touched on a playing card and she pulled it out. Frankie's last gift to her.

Emmie smiled and her eyes teared up. The Justice card.

GET BOOK 2 IN THE EMMIE ROSE HAUNTED MYSTERY SERIES on the next page and find out how to stay updated!

Read Book 2 on Amazon.com!

Caine House: An Emmie Rose Haunted Mystery Book 2

More books by Dean Rasmussen:

Dreadful Dark Tales of Horror Book 1
Dreadful Dark Tales of Horror Book 2
Dreadful Dark Tales of Horror Book 3
Dreadful Dark Tales of Horror Book 4
Dreadful Dark Tales of Horror Book 5
Stone Hill: Shadows Rising Book 1
Stone Hill: Phantoms Reborn Book 2
Stone Hill: Leviathan Wakes Book 3

PLUS, get a **FREE** short story at my website!

www.deanrasmussen.com

★★★★★
Please review my book!

https://www.amazon.com/dp/1951120177

If you liked this book and have a moment to spare, I would greatly appreciate a short review on the page where you bought it. Your help in spreading the word is *immensely* appreciated and reviews make a huge difference in helping new readers find my novels.

ABOUT THE AUTHOR

Dean Rasmussen grew up in a small Minnesota town and began writing stories at the age of ten, driven by his fascination with the Star Wars hero's journey. He continued writing short stories and attempted a few novels through his early twenties until he stopped to focus on his computer animation ambitions. He studied English at a Minnesota college during that time.

He learned the art of computer animation and went on to work on twenty feature films, a television show, and a AAA video game as a visual effects artist over thirteen years.

Dean currently teaches animation for visual effects in Orlando, Florida. Inspired by his favorite authors, Stephen King, Ray Bradbury, and H. P. Lovecraft, Dean began writing novels and short stories again in 2018 to thrill and delight a new generation of horror fans.

ACKNOWLEDGMENTS

Thank you to my wife and family who supported me, and who continue to do so, through many long hours of writing.

Thank you to my friends and relatives, some of whom have passed away, who inspired me and supported my crazy ideas. Thank you for putting up with me!

Thank you to my beta readers!

Thank you to all my supporters!

Made in the USA
Middletown, DE
23 October 2021